Mother
in the
Dark

Mother
in the
Dark

KAYLA MAIURI

RIVERHEAD BOOKS
New York
2022

RIVERHEAD BOOKS

An imprint of Penguin Random House LLC
penguinrandomhouse.com

Library of Congress Cataloging-in-Publication Data

Names: Maiuri, Kayla, author.
Title: Mother in the dark / Kayla Maiuri.
Description: New York : Riverhead Books, 2022.
Identifiers: LCCN 2021039252 (print) | LCCN 2021039253 (ebook) |
ISBN 9780593083284 (hardcover) | ISBN 9780593086421 (ebook)
Subjects: LCGFT: Fiction.
Classification: LCC PS3613.A35255 M68 2022 (print) |
LCC PS3613.A35255 (ebook) | DDC 813/.6—dc23
LC record available at https://lccn.loc.gov/2021039252
LC ebook record available at https://lccn.loc.gov/2021039253

Printed in the United States of America
1st Printing

Book design by Cassandra Garruzzo Mueller

For my mother and father

PART I

Everett, Massachusetts

1974

A girl steps through a sun-beat field, singing while she picks dandelions, dingy things, wild, but her mother's favorite. The field lies behind their house. It's mottled with weeds and tufts of grass. Broken bottles glitter and crunch underfoot. The girl, Diana, handles the flowers with grace, careful not to break the stems when she plucks and stows them in her canvas bag. Factories nearby thrum like a swarm of insects, and old New England homes breathe cloudy air through open windows. The girl sings with her mother, *ninna nanna, ninna nanna, baby's going ninna nanna*, as neighbors drink instant coffee behind the grainy blur of screened-in porches, voices traveling between houses like ghosts. She gathers and sings as she wanders across the vacant lot, past cigarette butts and paper bags, below the smeared contrail of a jet plane. She loses track of where her mother's voice is coming from, begins to hear it from several directions at once as she steps and stumbles over dry ground, the houses and factories shrinking to toy buildings she can pinch with her fingers, the flaming disc of the sun washing the field white. It's not until she reaches the chain-link fence that she realizes her mother is gone.

1

It's two in the morning and we're retelling our troubles until we discover something new. We do this every weekend in our Morningside Heights apartment. My underarms itch from sweat-laughing. Vera's eyes are crumby with day-old mascara. It's late November and the room feels close, cradling us in warmth and wine and yellow light.

"I know I say this all the time, but every person feels things differently. Copes differently. Like, something that's traumatic for you could be no issue for me," Vera says, downing the last of her cabernet. Our drunken talks always feel like revelations.

"Absolutely," I say. It's true that Vera's had more obstacles thrown in her path than most. I often wonder how she's learned to be shaped but not overcome by those experiences. I suspect she finds me self-pitying, that after all these years, she can't understand why I still dwell on my past. For the first time, it feels like she's telling me my feelings are legitimate.

Vera, my roommate and oldest friend. She's leaving tomorrow to meet her boyfriend's family in Des Moines. She calls Jonathan her boyfriend though she's known him for only five weeks. I don't know how she can stomach him—his vague pretense of having deep thoughts that are clearly plagiarized from a podcast, his long digressions about backpacking in Brazil. I'm not discreet about my feelings toward him, remaining stone-faced when he recites old movie lines. I don't applaud his De Niro impression. I don't smile.

I hate that she's so desperate for love.

Behind us, the pipes clang like there's someone trapped in the walls. That's what Vera and I say—that a frail, lost man is living with us. We call him Nathaniel, envision long arms and legs, a flattened torso that moves crabwise all around.

"I have to pee," she says. "But wait. I'm not done talking." This means she wants me to sit on the arm of the sofa while she goes to the bathroom with the door open. She lifts her nightgown to her belly button before she's made it to the toilet. I've known Vera for thirteen years and have lived with her for six. She almost never wears underwear, unless she's on her period. She's bald there now, since she's started seeing someone. I noticed her little hairs circling the shower drain this morning and couldn't help feeling jealous.

"Remember when I dated the married guy?" she asks.

"You mean, five months ago? Yes, Vera. I remember."

She laughs at herself. "I've been thinking about him."

Christian didn't tell Vera he was married. She was bombarded one morning with frantic voicemails from his wife, called a homewrecker and a slut, among other things. Vera cried a lot in those days, heavy tears that soaked her nightgown through. I held her for hours in bed, rubbed her back, told her to block his number and never reach out again. She continued to sneak around with him for weeks. There were many more shrieking calls from his wife, and when she started phoning Vera's office, Vera had no choice but to back off.

"Should I text him?" she whispers.

"Vera!" I scold, but there's a surge of excitement at the prospect of her cheating on Jonathan, leaving him, being single again with me.

"I know, I know. I'm only kidding."

We've downed two bottles of wine without pause. The hangover is creeping in. We continue to talk about the days of our youth as though we are sixty and not twenty-four.

Through the window, the benches are snowcapped, stippled with pigeon prints. Winter came early to New York. The apartments across the way glow shades of yellow. Figures move from room to room. They look like doll-people. I want to collect their love seats and kitchen sets, the paintings nailed to the floral walls. I want to keep them safe in the palm of my hand.

I catch sight of my face in the glass—tired, an afterthought impressed on the world. When I let out a yawn, Vera flushes the toilet and begins a new subject. She's trying to distract me from going to bed, from abandoning her, as she likes to put it.

"Ten more minutes," I say, knowing it will be twenty.

Soon we're in my bed with our heads on the same yellowed pillow. Vera pushes her bare ass cheek against my thigh and I scream, almost shoving her onto the floor. She lets out her wild laugh.

"One more time and you're out of here!" I say, not meaning it. I pretend to be annoyed, but the feeling of Vera pressed against me brings me a comfort I've only felt in childhood, since the days of sleeping in the same bed as my sisters.

We laugh until we're too tired to make any more noise. Vera flops onto her back. Our breathing slows. The room is dim except for the glow-in-the-dark star that clings to the ceiling.

"Where'd you get that?" she asks, as if she hasn't slept in this bed countless nights, staring up at that very star. She points to it with her chin. "How come there's only one?"

"Some guy gave it to me," I lie. In fact, I stole it from a party in Harlem at a friend of a friend's place. The apartment was hot and crowded, so I wandered deeper inside, looking for a space of my own. I landed in a closet-sized room with a shadeless lamp and a mattress on the floor, a single wall coated in stars. I peeled one off with my thumbnail and slid it into my purse.

"My mom wouldn't let us have those stars," I tell Vera. "I don't know why. She would have liked them."

"It's weird how you talk about your family," she says. "Like they're dead."

I choose not to respond, letting sleep take over. Next morning, I'm barely conscious when Vera slips out with her suitcase.

Now I'm alone in this cramped apartment that suddenly feels vast, as if the routes from my bedroom to the kitchen to the bathroom have stretched. Around six at night, when I can no

longer stand the loneliness, Nathaniel in the walls, I escape outdoors, welcoming the cold air down the neck of my coat, the way
it smooths the damp from my cheeks.

The cathedral across the way is stony and grand, out of place
in these cluttered, low-rise streets. In the night dark it's somehow
a shadow.

I wish I had something to do—a friend to meet or a shift at
the restaurant. Instead, I walk the fifty blocks down to Columbus Circle, touch the walled entrance to the park with my hand,
walk back, deliberately pound my heels on the pavement because
I like the way it sounds. In my open, flapping wool coat, boot-
laces clicking, I might look like a girl who knows where she's
going.

I imagine what Vera's plane ride to Iowa must have been
like—her sitting giddy, unwrapping her three-dollar headphones,
scanning through blockbuster films. She's only flown once or
twice. I wish it'd been me sitting beside her, gripping the same
armrest upon takeoff. By now she's probably surrounded by his
family, sitting in a warm den that's already decorated for Christmas. I'll bet they're wearing pajamas, drinking hot toddies or
cider. Maybe they're playing charades.

And what am I doing? I'm sweating and my left boot has
entirely eaten my sock. I bend to fish it out, when I get a call
from my sister. I let it ring. Aside from a few catch-up texts, Lia
and I haven't spoken in three months. I get a weird feeling when
she leaves a message. I play it right away.

Her voice is harried and upset, failing to hide the panic.

"Pick *up*," she says. I don't need to answer to know she's calling about my mother, to know something horrible has happened.

Call back, I tell myself. *You need to call back.* But my fingers won't dial.

O n Seventy-Eighth Street, colorful beanies dip as walkers pass, the tails of their scarves drifting. The crowd dissolves. I spot a man alongside the park, plump and mouth-breathing. Our eyes meet and he gestures toward his camera, points back to an impatient-looking woman whose arms are full of shopping bags. Beside her looms a pair of preteen girls wearing too much eyeliner, their mouths dragged into frowns. A photo of the four of them. This is all he wants.

I align the frame and the family inches closer, their hips touching, heads tilting toward one another. The mother's arms tremble as she grips the swollen bags. Behind them, a snowy Central Park gleams. I ignore the buzzing in my pocket, count down from three. That's when I spot a figure hobbling through the lens, a woman stooped over in a shapeless coat, red hair streaming onto her back in knots. Her body is curved, her shape hollowed into a comma. The resemblance is so uncanny, so disquieting; I have to pause. I don't realize I've focused the lens on her until I've handed the camera back.

The woman haunts me on my trek back to Morningside. Any semblance of a normal evening is wrecked. I look to the buildings and monuments to save me, to pull me out of my own head.

I haven't seen my mother in three years, since after college. The resentments have grown into something more, something menacing, strangling. I know she isn't well. I'm plagued by thoughts of losing her, visions of her slipping into death while on her way to sleep. My worries for her are not enough to send me back to her punishing silence, her invasive weakness.

She didn't see me off the morning I left. She looked up from her magazine to nod goodbye and that's how I remember her—sitting on the couch in her powder-blue nightgown, doodling in the margins of *Country Living*. She sat cross-legged with an iced coffee wedged in her lap, her nightgown riding up her thighs to expose the patch of black between her legs. When she caught me staring, she adjusted the coffee cup, not embarrassed. "Well, what the hell," she said, after I made a face. "Don't look, then."

By then, the summer I turned eighteen, she was living on the couch. I could have milked my sadness, warmed up to her. But I was almost free.

I didn't have any expectations when I came to New York—just the misty, haloed idea that it was where true life waited, where it was not absurd to be alone. It was a place where I could slip into invisibility. I believed the city could distract me from my haunts, make me wiser, raise me in a way she hadn't. Cure me.

She comes to me in the quiet.

In these apparitions, she is charismatic, magnetic, perpetually childlike as she tosses loaves of bread to the birds in our

Everett yard. I can see the fawn-colored freckles splayed across her face, the patch of white on her nose where the freckles disappear. I can smell the clean auburn hair that falls past her shoulders in waves. She is lovely in the dandelion sunlight—her gestures spirited when she talks to the birds like people. My younger sisters and I join her at the back door, our doughy noses pressed against the screen as we listen to the putts and clucks of the birds, their fights over clumps of bread. We're warm and at ease, caressed by the scent of her fresh cotton nightgown.

I can see her sitting in the old breakfast nook, surrounded by shelves of recipe books, decorative spoons, and Italian farm-girl figurines. She licks her fingers and presses them onto the oven tray, picking up popcorn-chicken crumbs. My father isn't there but there are traces of him: a yellow hard hat on the hallway bench, a can of peanuts, a fishing report. Lia sits on the chair beside my mother, reading books borrowed from the library truck—volumes on solar systems and sea creatures—used books with spines that crack. On the kitchen counter, my youngest sister, Sofia, paints sunny skies with her fingers.

It's easy for me to get lost in the shiny lacquer of childhood memories. There's a familiar pull—a feeling of regret or longing—the indescribable need to be back in that house. In my mind, we don't age. We're three scrubby-haired girls.

2

In my earliest memory, my mother is sitting on the beige carpet of the front parlor, watching the Game Show Network while she eats green olives from the jar. She slurps out a pimento pepper, swaying as she chews, pats an olive-stained leg to motion us over. I can't wait to be close to her, mush against her, rest my head in her lap and suck in her scent. Her sleeves smell of cold cream because she's just taken a bath. In the background, my sisters let out muted laughs; conversations I half remember and re-remember, memories I reconstruct.

We stand before her in our *Cinderella* nightgowns, Sofia clutching a bouquet of Q-tips. "Mummy, do our ears?" she asks, stretching the cotton swabs forward.

At this age, we're inseparable. The four of us fill an entire room. If one of us is absent, I can feel it.

We lived in Everett, across the water from Boston. The houses on our street were crammed in a row, indistinguishable, with matching paper cutouts in the windows—rosy-cheeked Santas in winter and bucktoothed bunnies in spring—and that same Virgin Mary statue mourning in the soil. Plastic windmills glinted in sunlight, in the tiny front yards gnawed away by concrete, each of them squared off with a chain-link fence.

There was always someone knocking on our door, someone stepping into the house unannounced, always a neighbor yelling from her porch to ours. On Sunday afternoons, the mothers offered leftover anginetti or pizzelle cookies, brought their children along. A group of us would play with our dolls in the front parlor, knocking their pretty heads together while the adults talked and drank tea or beers in the kitchen.

My mother grew up a few blocks away, and my father a few blocks farther from her. Everyone knew my mother, Little Dee, and she still joined the neighbors for scopa games and homemade-pizza nights, even when my father declined. In spring, she went with a group to the abandoned field to gather the sprouting dandelions. The older women tossed the flowers into their water-filled tubs to wash, and later ate the petals in salads. My mother placed the stems in stained-glass bottles, giving them a home on our windowsill.

When the weather warmed, she sent us to the porch with bleedy pomegranates, let us dig out the seeds with our fingers, spraying the wood. Our tiny street was populated with children who dipped flyswatters into buckets of soapy water and washed the concrete walls for fun. Sometimes, we peeked through the schoolyard fence to find the man with no arms eating grapes with his toes in his backyard. We used to think he couldn't see us through the dense shrubbery, but we were wrong. He performed for us, did tricks with his feet, kicked grapes into the air and caught them in his mouth.

On long summer nights, in the tacky heat, men and women lounged in thin cotton on their steps until dawn. They smoked packs of cigarettes, cooled the backs of their necks with Sam Adams bottles. I relished this closeness, calmed to sleep each night by the murmuring of others, voices I'd known since birth. I listened to their stories—tales of Italians immigrating to Boston, to this very street, with nothing but a passport and a single suitcase. Spaghetti westerns thwacked from every television. Connie Francis poured from stereos. No one bought pasta from the store; on Sundays, every surface in every house—tables, sofas, and beds—was covered in cookie sheets, where the mothers left their tagliatelle or pappardelle to dry. For days afterward, the scents of garlic and tomato lingered in the curtains.

Our house had water-stained ceilings and gummy wallpaper. It was full of primary colors; vibrant plastic toys lining the edges of every room, peeping out from carpet fibers. The banister wriggled when you grabbed on. There was a single bathroom for the five of us. I remember my mother having to sit on the pink toilet to blow-dry her hair while my father shaved over the sink. When not in use, the tub was filled to the brim with our dirty clothes because there was nowhere else to put them. There were exactly five chairs at the table. Guests, or us kids, would have to sit in the parlor for meals.

I shared a room with my sisters, and though we had our own beds, we pushed the three of them together to make one. When I was alone in that room, I liked to reach my hand outside the window and hold it flat against the blue clapboard siding of the neighbors' house, only a few feet away. I pretended this touch gave me the power to absorb their voices. I invented dialogue about needing to bathe the children or put the baby to bed, fantasized of a husband kissing his wife on the cheek.

When I think of those days, I picture my mother and her best friend, Debbie, sitting on the front porch with spiked lemonades, black knockoff shades shielding their faces. My mother lifts her hair from her shoulders, fans herself with the stack of mail she hasn't brought into the house yet. They're an odd couple—one short and fleshy, the other tall, rail thin. I watch them from my spot on the little patch of green, ripping the grass while my sisters prod at worms on the sidewalk. My mother is self-conscious, keeps stretching her shirt over her stomach to hide the pouch. Debbie lets her imperfections hang out, doesn't seem to care about things like that.

The tragedy of starting the first grade meant having to leave my mother. I woke each morning before the sun breached our bedroom window, my sisters pressed against all sides of me. So deep-rooted was my anxiety that I picked at the bunnied wallpaper behind the iron bedframe until I tore whole shreds away, exposing the dry wall, the color of mucus. While my father showered, I lay with my mother in their queen bed. She swathed me in her arms, let me nudge her with my knees so that her softness might absorb me. We established a patient routine, a mock-happy variation on certain phrases and consolations—*the other girls say goodbye to their mothers, you have to be a big girl for your sisters*. The repetition, the slowing of time in those moments, offered me something like relief. While resting in her arms, I thought of drastic ways to hide. There were the garbage bins in the backyard, the child-sized gap beneath the neighbors' porch. Mostly, though, I willed time to stop. I clung to consciousness in those early hours, afraid to fall asleep again, to wake only to be torn from her.

Once my mother was dressed and a neighbor had come by to watch my sisters, we'd take the walk to school, the same school my mother had gone to as a child. It was an endless, tearful march past the fences with morning glories sprouting through the pickets, past construction workers eating breakfast sandwiches—their hands and knees white with plaster—past the abandoned factories and housing projects, all the way to the Mystic River.

Our love for our mother never faltered. She was our savior, nearly mythic. At ages seven, nine, and ten, my sisters and I treasured afternoons alone with her, weekends when our father traveled down the East Coast for fishing trips. It was a space reserved for us. We orbited our mother, taken in by her spell—a mood of silky, dreamy content. She was the most beautiful woman we'd ever seen, wearing her hair in loose ponytails with strands gracefully framing her cheeks. Gold hoops dangled from her ears. In certain lights, the costume gems in her second holes gleamed.

On those weekends, our father was not outside laying mulch or in the front parlor with his blueprints spread across the floor.

There was no one around to keep us in line. We danced around the house our mother ruled.

The ceiling fan blew warm air around the kitchen. A pot of red sauce crackled and plumed while she hummed a song from childhood—a mix of Italian and English words. My sisters and I spun on our toes, wove dish towels in the air. We climbed onto chairs to stand above the pot, to let the sweet tomato steam moisten our faces. My mother wiped a sponge across the table, suds dripping to the floor in iridescent shines, spraying the tile. *Ninna nanna, ninna nanna, baby's going ninna nanna.* I felt intense delight as her hands pulled mine into the warm bucket of water. The smell of soapy lemons filled the room as we swished the table together. I wanted to live in that space forever, isolated and unchanging.

There was a shift in the air when he came through the door. At the sound of his steps, my sisters and I dispersed, floated apart. Sawdust followed him into the house. A wetness clung to his upper lip. I could smell him from across the room, spiced and bitter, could almost detect the scent of packaged pastries he'd sneakily devoured in his truck. He bought them at the corner store each day, factory-made sticky buns and coffee cakes, sickly sweet.

My father was thickly built but moved slowly, lumbering because of the twinges in his lower back. Some nights he lay facedown on the cool kitchen tile, trying to relieve the pain. My mother would shift the small television on the counter so he could watch his baseball games from the floor. She receded into the background, tender but detached, in the room with us but entirely alone.

3

My mother's downfall began on a Tuesday, the rain-dimmed morning my father made the announcement. He ushered us all into the family room, where we hopped on the stained blue sofa, kicked our legs as we ate salami-and-cheese roll-ups. My mother sat between us like a fourth sister, unsuspecting, coffee steaming from her Charlie Brown mug. The downpour rushed like blood in our ears.

My father was talking to the dog, rubbing him with a socked foot. "Hey, little man," he said, with an intimacy reserved just for him. Beans, a terrier mix who was almost fourteen, deaf and blind, coughed damply.

"Come on, Vin," my mother said. "I'm growing grays over here." With her thumb and forefinger, she wiped coffee from her mouth, brushed a few crumbs from her nightgown. There was something comical about the tidying gesture, given what was about to happen.

My father fake coughed, rubbed his palms together so they made a muted sandpapery sound I hated. He was suntanned year-round from the hours he spent supervising rooftops and construction sites, his Sicilian skin taut and thirsty.

Before the new school year, he explained, we would move out of our run-down town house and into a *real* home—one with four bedrooms, air-conditioning, and a sink that didn't smell like eggs when you twisted the faucet. There would be a yard in front and out back, a driveway, wide expanses of land between houses where we could roam and play. It was a new adventure, my father said, an hour away, in the country.

"What do we think?" he asked, as if waiting for a real answer. His expectant gaze bounced between the four of us, and from the way he eyed my mother, whose lips were parting in a look of surprise, I suspected he didn't have her support.

We stirred, made shy buzzing sounds. I fixated on the sofa cushion that was riddled with food stains and blemishes, a tiny no-necked man that Lia had drawn in permanent marker. I was skeptical, but tried to feel comforted by my father's woody after-shave and slicked-back hair, his palpable certainty.

The idea of leaving this house brought me a feeling I couldn't place, a subtle sorrow for the oil-slicked walls and chipped cabinet knobs we'd be leaving behind. I couldn't articulate this to my father. Something about his eager expression aroused a feeling like pity. We'd learn later that he'd been showing his drawings around the North Shore, that he'd been hired to design and build each of the homes in a new subdivision, employ the contractors, oversee the construction. "We're getting first pick," he said proudly. "The biggest lot in the development."

It was dead quiet in the family room. An airy sound when the old pipes clicked on, as if they were stretching, cracking their joints.

My mother's tongue probed the inside of her cheek. "So, it's done, then."

He raised his eyes to look at her. They had a sort of staring contest. Then my mother pushed off the couch, her coffee flying from her lap, confirming that this was the first time she was hearing the news. I accepted this as a life decree I was just now learning—that husbands made decisions without wives, that mothers could be ruled like children. "What the hell is this, Vin? You said we'd decide together. You promised me."

"Dee," he called out, his voice searching but firm. "Diana." I'd never heard him say her full name.

She fled, ignoring my father. On the carpet, her mug lay smashed. Charlie Brown broken to pieces. Coffee seeped and I was sure I could hear the rug slurping it up.

Outside, the traffic heightened. Car tires droned on the wet street and exhaust billowed up the first-floor windows. Upstairs, my mother slammed a door.

My father waved for us to follow and we joined her on the big bed, where she lay belly-up with the fan going, a pillow over her face. Unused to this behavior from our mother, we stood idly on either side of her.

He turned it into a game, trying to lure her from beneath the pillow, prodding, tickling her feet. We joined in, laughing as we poked at her sides from every direction. She was small and round, unable to dodge our mighty jabs. We pushed and nudged, rolled up our dirty socks and stuffed them under the pillow. "Stop it," she squealed. Her fingers grasped at the fabric. I worried for whether she could breathe. She moaned and stirred, swatting us away. Eventually, we left her. I don't think any of us realized how upset she was.

My mother was raised in a dilapidated two-family home on a polluted street that was rampant with coughing neighbors, all battling some strange illness. They blamed it on the Monsanto Chemical Co. burying toxin-filled barrels underground, which later eroded, letting the cancer leak out. That house was a ten-minute walk from ours. I'd been inside it only once, when I was seven or eight, after my grandfather Giuseppe died and we needed to clear out his things. I have little memory of Nonno. He was from Naples and proud of his heritage, bickering with the neighbors about who made a better calamari plate, the Neapolitans or the Sicilians. He used to walk the first floor of our house, jingling the coins in his pockets and singing:

> *Ma n'atu sole*
> *cchiù bello, oi ne'.*
> *'O sole mio*
> *sta 'nfronte a te!*
> *'O sole, 'o sole mio*
> *sta 'nfronte a te,*
> *sta 'nfronte a te!*

I couldn't believe my mother had lived in such a place, with long curtains posing as doors, with the floors so slanted that objects freely rolled from one end of the room to the other. In

the cellar, patches of moss swarmed on the walls. Baby mush-
rooms sprouted from concrete.

"They used to pump the chemicals right into the Mystic
River," my mother said, walking us through the tiny rooms. "It
used to shine rainbow colors and Nonno and his brothers would
swim in it. They didn't know any better," she said, peering out
the window. "I'll end up dying of some weird disease."

"Don't tell them that, Dee."

"It's the truth. When I was a kid, everyone was always talking about it. How you couldn't leave your windows open or else
there'd be an inch of sulfur on your surfaces the next morning—
your bureau, your kitchen counters. If you took in a deep breath,
you'd start choking. That was from the power plants." She
stopped again at the window. The field was torn up, missing
patches of grass. "In the summer, groups of boys used to throw
matches in the grass and it'd burn blue and green." She smiled.
"The power plants would start spewing after supper and the
mothers would yell from their porches, 'Come inside, the poi-
son's coming!' Imagine that?" She laughed, shaking her head.

My sisters and I shared a look.

"You should try spending a night in this place," she said,
scuffing at the dirtied tile. "The nights were brutal. Trying to fall
asleep in the heat. Nonna used to hear me rustling in bed and
she'd wave me into the kitchen. We'd grab handfuls of sugar
from the jar and kneel on the floor, lure the mice. She loved the
critters," my mother said. "Nonno used to smash them with the
broom."

Something about the scene unsettled me—the inherent

closeness between mother and daughter, the irrefutable likeness, the smushed mice.

I never knew my mother's mother, Marilena. She died years before I was born, and my mother still grieved about it. Sometimes, I caught her late at night on the porch, looking down the street or up at the stars, talking to her, asking her where she'd been.

She came to me in the night. I'd wake in half sleep to find my grandmother, a woman I'd only seen in photographs, standing above my bed. A phantom of my mother's past. She wore the same nightgowns as my mother—silky and to the knee. Sometimes, my mother stood beside her, their faces milky white from the moon's cast. When I tried to reach for them, my arms wouldn't move.

With our mother cooped up in her room, my sisters and I traded paint swatches at the table, begging our father to tell us how big our bedrooms would be, how many windows they'd have, if there were any secret spaces or hidden doors. He pulled out the blueprints and laid them in front of us, the new house becoming more tangible in our minds, as though we were the ones building it. When she heard the pizza delivery, our mother came down. She sat at the other end of the table, rolling paper napkins into snakes. She eyed the pizza but wouldn't reach for a slice, depriving herself to make some kind of point.

"A little spoiled, no?" She finally spoke. "Giving them their own rooms?"

We each lowered our paint swatches, peered reassuringly at

our father for an answer. I felt a hint of rage at the thought of her ruining this for us.

"Lots of kids have their own rooms," he said.

"Not around here they don't."

She was right about this. We'd been to almost every house on the block. Siblings slept together in twin trundle beds or sometimes one big mattress, except for the baby, who had its own room, the size of a closet.

"Nothing good's going to come from this," she said.

Perhaps things would have turned out differently had he pitched the move to her privately, pretended her opinion mattered. She often joked that he loved us more than he loved her, that she was the last priority. As the years progressed, this became less of a joke and more of an accusation.

He'd forced her to get her driver's license some months earlier, despite her being terrified and having decided it wasn't for her. There wasn't much of a motive, aside from it being dangerous to walk to school in winter on the ice. We understood now that he'd been thinking about the new town. She would need to drive us from the school, to the playground, to the grocery store. There weren't even any sidewalks.

He begged her to take a ride with him out there, to the new house, to witness its various stages—the pouring of the foundation, the rising of the beams and walls. My mother refused, so we girls joined him. It was exciting, standing in the middle of the half-built house, inhaling the honeyed scent of sawdust and the promise of something new. I loved the thud of my sneakers on freshly planted floorboards, the ashy swipe of plaster on my fingertips. We swore to our mother that she'd love it if she would only see it.

"It's in the woods," she said. "I hate the woods."

"It won't be for long," my father said, drawing a map on a napkin. "There will be other houses going up. A nice cul-de-sac where you can plant flowers."

She scoffed.

"There'll be lots of animals. We know you're a crazy bird lady," he said, trying to make her laugh.

"Who's going to visit us up there?"

"You'll meet new people. The girls will go to a great public school. One of the best."

My mother dreaded the isolation, the dense quiet of suburbia—the idea that everyone was watching but wouldn't dare cross their lawn to greet you. "We won't fit in, in a place like that," she'd told my sisters and me when my father was out of earshot.

4

In the weeks after the announcement, I spent long nights with her in the front parlor as her chosen confidante. She kept me up with stories I was too young to hear—family myths and secrets, loyalties and betrayals. She quieted at the mention of Nonna, except to say that she'd put my father in his place if she were here. "She didn't let anyone tell her what to do."

Sleepless nights fueled by my mother left me exhausted come morning. "Don't you start yawning in front of your teachers," she'd say. "They'll think I'm a bad mother." I spent the first hours of school with my teeth clenched, afraid for a yawn to escape.

We were on the couch one Sunday when suddenly she spilled her coffee in my lap. It emptied onto me with a hot hiss. I screamed, wailed as the coffee soaked, fusing cotton to skin. She didn't react right away. It was my father who swooped me in his arms and ran me to the kitchen sink, where my feet collided with greasy pots and pans. He punched the faucet on, drenched napkins, and wrapped them around my thighs, ignoring the water that spilled over the counter, darkening the kitchen grout. I followed the stream of tap water to my mother, who stood behind my father, pacing. Beads of coffee dripped from her fingertips, drying on her skin in watercolor streaks. Her arms drifted from her sides as she advanced. A creature from the deep.

It was March, and then April. As the move approached, my mother kept retreating. Her response to the upcoming move was to make herself immovable. Each day, something new seemed altered, undone. Her hair became matted. The flesh around her eyes puckered. Lines of tension were etched on her forehead and the edges of her mouth. It seemed she'd aged a generation in a few weeks. When she smiled, only one cheek went up, as if there were something darker swarming around in her brain.

She abandoned most of her duties as the stay-at-home parent, refusing to come downstairs even in the needy hours before school. She stopped joining us for meals, stowed pistachios and shredded wheat in the pockets of her robe, snacked during the day. Scattered on the floor by her bed were apple cores, string cheese wrappers, and cans of Italian-style tuna. Mugs of curdled milk and tea littered her nightstand. Beside them lay ceramic bowls caked with bananas and oatmeal.

In the corner of the room stood an empty birdcage, where the parakeets lived, the bottom of the enclosure covered with old newspaper and gravel, droppings and crimped feathers. Within weeks of my mother falling into her strange, slow mood, the birds were gone.

Vanished was the mother who once appeared at my bedside, listening to my worries, who unburdened me before sleep. She used to wake us by spelling words on our backs with soft fingers:

R-I-S-E-A-N-D-S-H-I-N-E. I could still hear the gold bangles clinking when they slid down her arm, could feel the covers swooping over my body.

I needed her to come back to me. I missed the sound of her rummaging in her pocketbook. I loved that first plunge—her long nails scraping the leather interior, clinking against pens, lipsticks, and hair clips, keys jingling. These sounds attributed purpose to my mother, responsibility. Now her pocketbook sat limp on the bedroom floor, its contents untouched. It was one month earlier that she was running around with energy and purpose. She'd been in charge of putting together the prizes for the town hall raffle—five dazzling wicker baskets, each with a different theme, packed with gardening tools or cooking supplies, wrapped in iridescent cellophane. The night was an enormous success. The town praised her creative eye. I'd never seen my mother that proud, invigorated.

At the time, I thought I knew about sadness. What it felt like to cry after a screaming match with your sisters, to be told you couldn't go somewhere, like the public swimming pool at the end of the street. I recalled moments in which I'd banged an elbow against a counter, the shock more intense than the pain, thinking this must have been what my mother's ailments were like. In truth, I understood little about her. She remained secluded in her room behind a door clicked shut. It was odd carrying on like nothing had changed, but we had to keep up our routine. I set my alarm clock to six each morning without

complaint, scrounging up food for our school lunches and preparing my younger sisters for the bus. When it was cold, and
with some coaxing, I'd manage to wake my mother so she could
drop us at the bus stop some blocks over.

There were a few events prior to my father's announcement that
seemed insignificant at the time, but they troubled me, as though
they foreshadowed a shift in our lives.

The most unnerving is what happened to our neighbor Leo.
My father used to have long talks with him under the flickering
porch light about local elections and baseball games. They
smoked cigars and cheersed beer bottles, took turns flinging
pretzels at a nail on the wall. We called Leo a grizzly bear because of his dark, furred forearms, the full head of locks that
stuck out of his cap. He was a towering but gentle Italian with
poison-green eyes. Around bedtime, my sisters and I would
sneak down barefoot for a kiss good night and Leo pretend-
roared, tickled us, and rustled our hair.

When my father was sixteen, Leo gave him his first job reno-
vating a three-story brownstone in Southie. My father used to
tell me about this—how when the plaster cured it released so
much heat and moisture it felt like working in a sauna. Sometimes, my father helped Leo install Sheetrock with screw guns.
Other days, he mixed the plaster. At the end of each shift, when
my father was cleaning the tools, his skin would slowly peel from
his hands because of the silica sand he had in the mix for the
textured ceilings. "Leo was an artist," my father said. The scroll-

work took skill and talent. He'd use a sponge attached to a trowel and, with a continuous figure-eight pattern, create whorls in the ceiling.

Of course, he couldn't do that anymore. One afternoon, Leo was palming leaves from the roof gutters when he tumbled to the driveway and cracked open his skull. Split it like a cantaloupe, as my mother put it. He hadn't been the same since.

After the accident, we'd often hear Leo wailing from inside his house—a deep, strangled howl that made me sick. Like he was seeing something that we couldn't, some encroaching horror no one could rescue him from. When his cries got too loud, my mother made us close the windows. She'd shake her head and lift her shoulders as if to say, *What can we do?*

I was waiting in the kitchen one morning before school, listening to the familiar clank of metal on pavement while a neighbor tinkered with their Ford pickup. Someone pelted a wet cough into a handkerchief. A few doors down, cigarette-busted voices cackled.

There was something rotting in the kitchen. I pushed down the mountain of trash to stifle the smell, but the barrel was filled to the brim. An empty pudding cup fell onto the floor.

"Anna, don't we have to leave?" Lia asked, pointing to the microwave clock. Her black hair fell past her eyes, which were doubly hidden by her thick-rimmed glasses. She wore a fuchsia windbreaker with a Hawaiian-print backpack, ready to go.

"Here," I said. "Take these." I handed each of my sisters a

baggie with two rice cakes inside, pressed together with peanut butter.

"I hate rice cakes," said Sofia, holding the baggie outstretched with two fingers. "They don't taste like anything." She was wearing a pink turtleneck and princess underwear, a fleece blanket wrapped lazily around her legs to keep warm. Her baby-soft hair was still pulled into yesterday's pigtails.

"It's all we have," I said. The contents in my own brown bag: a soft clementine that was spotted, a granola bar crumbled inside the wrapper.

Sofia groaned and slumped away. The blanket dragged behind her, collecting crumbs and plastic wrappers. She still needed my mother's help to get dressed.

"Why doesn't she go shopping?" Lia said, more a statement than a question. She was only two years older than Sofia, but the no-nonsense inflection in Lia's voice made her seem older. She boosted herself onto her toes, rested her chin on the kitchen island.

Whenever we claimed to be hungry, our mother laughed, her teeth showing like dirty pearls. "Hungry? You should've seen what I ate when I was your age. We never had food. Nonno used to make me steal." She smiled at her misfortune, wearing it like a badge. "He used to take me to the peanut butter factory. He'd lift me by the armpits and I'd slip my arms right through the window bars, grab handfuls of peanuts. Fill my pockets right up. You girls don't know what hungry is."

I opened the fridge once more, hoping something edible might appear. There was only a bag of red grapes and a wilting cucumber, a yellow-brown substance congealing on the shelf. Everything else needed to be cooked.

"Come on," I said. "Let's see if she's up."

From the open bottle on the counter, I shook four pills into my palm. They were for my mother's migraines, which I knew were coming when she massaged the single vein that bulged from her temple. More and more, she was waking up with them. The headaches were recent, spawned from restless nights spent choking and panting for air. She'd wake up the whole house.

"Maybe give her five more minutes?" Lia asked, tugging my dress. She was afraid to go up there.

"We don't *have* five more minutes. Come on."

I crept down the hall to where my mother slept, rapped my knuckles against the peeling doorframe. I led my sisters into darkness, the olive-green carpet swallowing our footsteps.

The room was frigid and gray, filled with the odor of dank rug. The curtains, once white, had turned a muddy beige. They ballooned at the open windows on either side of the four-poster bed, where mildewed beach towels, peach and pinstriped, were hung to conceal the sun. My mother's figure lay cloaked in shadow, still and noiseless. Beans had his back pressed against hers, legs stretched out. His eyes peeped open and he fell back to sleep.

"What's that smell?" Sofia plugged her nose.

"Quiet," I said, scuffing her head with my palm.

One step deeper into the room. The smell was coming from our mother's body, her nightgown, yellowed with sweat. It mingled with the scent of baby powder, which she applied nightly after her bath. I loved to watch the waft of white drifting from her hands and floating like a cloud around her pubic hairs.

"Mom," I whispered. When she didn't respond, I used her real name. "Diana."

Her eye twitched but she didn't wake.

Each of us slid onto the mattress, tugged the duvet to our chins. We listened to our mother's breathing, labored and slow. I drew circles on the sheets with my unclipped nails, the pills melting in my palm, smearing pink. An airy whistle as the towel-curtains flapped. I pictured life outside the windows—the hibernating dogwoods lining the road, and behind them, the Mystic River that popped and groaned beneath thawing ice.

I poked a finger into her backside, soft, like pressing into a sponge. None of us liked to be the one to wake her. I poked once more—this time with force.

She gasped and heaved to life, eyes wildly searching the room. "What the hell," she said, her voice thick from sleep. "You didn't have to come in like a bunch of sneaks!" She looked older, washed-out and distressed, the terry cloth of her robe the same ashen hue as her skin.

"We were letting you sleep," I said, feigning innocence.

My sisters sat up, smoothing their hair to get rid of the static.

I held my palm open and she snatched the damp pills, swallowed them dry.

My mother was smaller then, the smallest I ever saw her. When she fell back on the bed, her breasts flattened and sagged into her armpits. The mattress caved. Her leg accidentally bumped mine and she scowled, kicked, and mumbled something about moving over. I had to use all my strength to keep from tumbling into her.

"God help me," she said to the ceiling. "What did I ever do to you?"

"We're going to miss the bus," I said firmly, with authority.

"Your sister's not even dressed," she said. "Oh, just walk to the stop. You have legs."

She pulled the blankets over her head and rolled onto her side, scattering the balled-up tissues that had flattened beneath her back. She was allergic to the guinea pig my father bought us that Christmas. It made her eyes turn pink, so she dabbed them with wet pieces of toilet paper, leaving trails of crumpled tissue around the house.

"There's not enough time to walk. Also, there's no food," I said.

"I'm sick," my mother said, in her little-girl voice. "I don't know what's wrong with me. Your father doesn't care." Her voice grew muddled as she spoke into the pillow. "I'm going to end up like what's-her-face down the street. Dawn La Rosa. Her husband didn't find her body in the bed until twelve hours later."

Each night, my father lectured her as he flipped through the *Family Medical Guide* on her nightstand—a reference book for naming each new illness. He believed the pain in her head, in her feet, and in her shoulders was a result of her sedentary lifestyle. When I first heard the word, I thought he'd said "sedimentary," which I'd recently learned about in school, and I imagined my mother's insides accruing soil and rocks.

"Where does it hurt?" I asked. In those early days, I longed to comfort her. As the oldest daughter, it was my duty. I tried my best to impersonate my father, my eyes taking in her body from head to toe, examining her, trying to spot the soreness.

She shook her head, like it was too painful to speak. "All over."

"Why don't you take some more medicine?"

"Just skip a day. Please."

"I have a grammar test," I said. "Sofia missed school yesterday. We don't want to skip."

Lia shifted to the top of the bed and leaned against the headboard; her legs crossed adult-like at the ankles. Sofia gripped the knob of the white closet door, swinging it from side to side.

"Skip and we'll do something nice," my mother said, her voice falling soft. "We'll make those crafts we bought."

"What do we say when the school calls?" Lia asked, considering it.

I slid off the bed. "Let's go, Lia. We'll run to the stop."

She spoke louder. "What do we say, Mom?"

"If the phone rings, don't pick up," she replied.

Sofia applauded silently, her body tense with glee.

Usually, I could rely on Lia to support me. She and I were Irish twins, born less than a year apart, and we sometimes bragged about this to Sofia. It worked out for Sofia in the end. She was used to exclusion, born into it. No amount of teasing seemed to bother her, and if it did, she'd just as quickly turn back to what she was doing. Sofia didn't take on as much as the rest of us, an upside to being the youngest.

"Go downstairs," my mother said, her voice almost smiling. "I'll be down in a bit."

In seconds, my sisters had dashed out of the room, Lia flinging her coat and backpack on the staircase landing, Sofia skipping around in her underwear. I began to protest but my mother was already dozing, mouth slack against the pillow.

Something about this sad creature, this new and other mother, felt terrifyingly familiar already.

While she rested and waited for the meds to kick in, the three of us colored in front of the television. I heard a clicking sound coming from Sofia, saw something blue rolling around in her mouth. She was always making me nervous, walking around chewing bottle caps or beaded bracelets, anything that would fit between her teeth. "Sofia. Spit it out. You're going to choke."

"Don't tell me what to do."

"You're like a dog."

Lia laughed.

Sofia rolled out her tongue, letting the thing drop on the carpet. A marker cap.

Around noon, our mother appeared downstairs in the family room entryway, a bedspread wrapped around her like a cape, her eyes half closed. She'd painted her mouth a rich, terra-cotta red. Lipstick bled from the corners of her smile, as if she had changed her mind and sponged it with the back of her hand. She was beautiful, but more and more, she took on childlike mannerisms;

I imagined a tiara placed lopsided on her head, the heels of her feet slipping out of too-big shoes. Beans loped around her as she stooped to her knees, sinking down among us on the floor.

"Little monkeys," she said languorously, as if she were drawing the words from her mouth with her fingertips. She pulled the blanket over our bodies, singing with affected tenderness. "You wanted to stay home with your mother?"

My ribs pressed into the ground beneath her load. She kissed the tops of our heads.

There was a knock on the door. My mother inhaled. "Stay quiet," she said, holding a finger to her lips. We twisted to look up at her, indignant, and she tried to hold us down. The bell rang.

"I can't breathe," Sofia said, her mouth squashed against the carpet.

We squirmed and wriggled out from under her, tiptoed to the front of the house.

"You're supposed to be in school," my mother hissed. "Don't let her see you!"

Standing on the front porch with two iced coffees and a Dunkin' Donuts bag was Debbie, my mother's closest friend.

"God help me," my mother said.

Older than my mother, somewhere in her forties, Debbie was harsh-looking but hypnotic, with unplucked golden brows and pores on her cheeks that resembled the speckled grain of orange peel, teeth the color of cloudy ice. Tiny lines grazed the edges of her puckered mouth, dry from smoking too many cigarettes. Her hair was usually uncombed, thick and straw-colored, growing down to her navel. She never carried a purse but stuffed her wallet in the back pocket of her boot-cut jeans, the denim stretched and faded. She was a freak for holiday sweaters— sequined jack-o'-lanterns in fall, cotton-ball snowmen in winter. Today she wore a spring T-shirt, baby chicks peeping their heads out from Easter eggs.

"Mom, it's just Debbie," Lia said.

"No shit it's Debbie. I'm not blind. Get over here."

We ignored her, kneeling below the windows in the foyer. The house was dark and cave-like; Debbie couldn't have spotted our figures without peering deeply through the glass. She re-adjusted the coffee tray, pulled on the yellowed bra strap that slipped down her arm.

"Why are we hiding from Debbie?" Lia asked.

"I don't want to deal with her," my mother said flatly.

"She has coffees and doughnuts," said Sofia.

"They aren't for you. She doesn't know you're here."

My mother's face reddened as her friend walked back to her car. She palmed her nightgown, patted down her hair. I'd never seen her do that with Debbie.

5

Back in the apartment, I fall onto the couch without turning on the lights, without removing my jacket or boots. Vera's fringed blue scarf hangs on a vintage cane chair we found on a sidewalk in Park Slope. My phone lies on the cushion beside me, its bright cover taunting. *Make the call.* My hands won't move to grab it.

What does my mother look like now? She is probably larger, using midnight snacks to cope. I imagine congested arteries and weakened lungs, airways that collapse during sleep. But what else has changed? How much has her skin slackened? Has she gone fully gray?

I almost call Vera but stop myself. I don't want Jonathan hearing about it, thinking he knows me. I bring my phone into the bedroom and place it on the bureau so that it's not too close, but not too far away. For the next several hours, I watch a medical drama on a laptop propped on my knees, chewing on oatmeal until I slip the spoon between my lips and there's nothing there but metal.

Through the window behind my bed, dawn begins its routine. My neighbors are still stirring with the energy of night animals as they talk politics on the balcony. I can hear their voices beneath my window, their glasses tapping on the wrought-iron table, their chairs scraping the concrete. They've been going at it all night—smoking, arguing—alcohol warming their throats until they can't feel the cold.

The apartment is stifling, exposed pipes ticking and spurting. My bed is lumpy with books and half-empty water bottles. I kick them to the bottom, listen to the crinkle. I hear another phantom phone ring, a sound that stops each time I lift my head.

Outside, one of the neighbors begins a story about the subway, a drunken night when he fell asleep on the Q train and woke up in Coney Island. His back pocket was cut from his jeans, his wallet stolen. The audience gasps. I can tell by his voice that he thinks he's charming, seductive, a good storyteller. The others ambush him with questions:

"What position were you sleeping in?"

"But didn't you feel him cutting your pants?"

"Wouldn't someone have stopped him?"

This is my chance to include myself, shout down from the window. Rising from the bed, I only pretend to participate, standing in front of my finger-streaked mirror unclothed, using elaborate hand gestures, talking and nodding.

No one asks the question I want to ask.

How do you know it wasn't a woman?

During the day, I sleep sporadically but deeply, pressed firmly against the mattress as I wait to be swallowed whole. With Vera gone, there is no one to distract me from sleeping the weekend away, sinking into the deep dark until there's nothing but reality scraps—faint whistles and shoe skids coming from the hall, running faucets, the closing of other tenants' doors. And I'm drowned in sheets. A quiet horror when half of me wakes but the rest of me can't move, numbed limbs that can only give in to the collapse.

Hours later, I wake in the late afternoon, too warm, brain fogged. It takes several seconds for my eyes to adjust to the line drawings thumbtacked to my wall—silhouettes of lounging women, a young couple embracing. It takes a full minute for my ears to register that the loud whirring sound is the fridge. I can hear ghostly Nathaniel moving through the walls, heading toward the kitchen. When I make a half effort to rise, my head pulls to one side. Every part of me feels weighted. The puddle stain on my pillow has grown—I went to bed with wet hair. When was the last time I washed my sheets? They've pilled and smell of musk. The rosebud design has faded to almost nothing.

Anxiety shrinks as the sun comes through the single curtain, is replaced by something else, shame, guilt. I lie on my back, on

my side. I close my eyes and open them. I flip through the paper-
back that's been on my nightstand for months—a novel by a
Hungarian author whose name I can't pronounce.

The pastry shop around the corner is comforting with its
framed book jackets and glossy white mugs, its bathroom stall
graffitied with philosophy quotes and the requisite penises. It's a
bustling place where the writing students from Columbia con-
vene. They talk about their novels-in-progress, have impassioned
discussions about Gaitskill or Morrison or Carver. The windows
are patterned with flyers for Arabic and piano lessons, names
and numbers of tutors and nannies, making me feel like I'm a
part of something bigger.

It's near empty, though. A young woman, her black hair
looped in a bun, reads *Eleven Kinds of Loneliness* in the corner. I
sit at a table beside her, try to mimic her posture. An elegant-
seeming person, she wears a long black dress and ankle-hugging
boots, no tights despite the cold. Her sleeves are pushed to her
elbows, her forearms and knuckles baring patches of white, some
kind of paint. This hint of sloppiness is surprising, alluring. It
doesn't go with the formal black dress. She compliments the
gold bracelet that clinches my wrist, sending a rush of warmth
through me. She returns to her book. I order a croissant because
it's my favorite thing to eat, even at the end of the day, when the
pastry is stale and I struggle to bite through it. I rip it into flaky
strips, dunk them into my coffee until it spills over. Several
minutes pass, then the woman hooks her tote on her arm, drops

some crumpled bills on the counter, and leaves. It catches me by surprise—her not saying goodbye. I leave a handful of sour dimes and nickels by my empty mug, go back to the park. On my walk home, I look for the stooped woman, the woman with tangled red hair, but she isn't there.

6

The spring he announced the move, there was little sign of my father's presence in the house, save for the pan of eggshells in the kitchen sink. Each morning, he left before the sun rose. I woke to his headlights swiping across our bedroom window like a giant wave goodbye.

I was always waiting for him to get fed up, to leave us, was always worrying about what would happen to us when he did. I resisted becoming my mother's ally, despite my father beginning to show his neglect. Keeping us home from school was her way of preserving the world she was afraid of losing—peopled, busy, full of the familiar rhythms and patterns of activity and closeness. I knew my father would not be happy if he found out. But I was sad for my mother. She had no one to talk to. She'd been avoiding her friends in the neighborhood for weeks, including Debbie. It was a way of proving her misery to my father.

He made a big commotion coming into the house one night, tossing his blueprints and briefcase on the counter, shuffling through the mail. Beans lay on the floor, all crusted joints and gray hairs. He started panting when my father walked in. "Old

man" we called Beans, because of his collapsing trachea, the re-
pulsive sound of every breath. I hated being in the same room
as him.

"What's all over the granite?" my father asked. "It's sticky."

"Must be duck sauce," my mother said, without turning from
the cutting board. "The girls had leftover Chinese." Bits of pork-
fried rice lay hardened on the granite.

My father rested his knuckles on the countertop as he studied
the back of my mother's head. She'd swapped the bathrobe for
black pants and an unraveling black sweater. "Are you going to
clean it?" he asked.

"What do I look like, the friggin' maid?" She turned to face
him, looking for a fight. Her hair was scraped back so tightly her
brows were upright, unmoving. Concealer was smeared beneath
her eyes, the color of cake batter.

He opened a tub of almonds and started crunching.

I went over to the blueprints, unzipped the pencil pouch.
"Dad, can I help you color the fire alarms?" I held his pink high-
lighter proudly in the air, letting him know I paid attention. I
knew the fire alarms were marked in pink.

He plucked his hat off, ran a hand through his ink-black hair.
"Not now, honey," he said. "I just got in." He rounded the
kitchen, pausing at Sofia. "What are you up to, little monkey?"

"Playing Clue," she said, in a drawn-out baby voice.

"You winning?"

"Mhm. Daddy?" Sofia said.

"Whatty?"

"Roll it." She held her palm open to show him the die. He gave it a toss and moved her piece five spaces.

"How was school?" he asked the room, cupping another handful over his mouth.

Before we could lie, our mother did. "Everyone had stomachaches today," she said. "Had to stay home."

"Stomachaches," he repeated.

"That's right."

I stole a look at my mother, who didn't seem the least bit nervous.

"Didn't Sofia miss school yesterday?"

My mother rinsed a rotting cucumber under the tap.

"Dee."

Please don't let anything bad happen. I slumped in my chair and crossed my fingers, repeating the words I believed would protect us. I did this when I felt we were in danger, or when my father came home at odd hours, climbing the stairs on all fours like a bear—when he made moaning, gurgling sounds, sometimes counting the steps. As a child, I didn't understand his drunkenness. I thought that was how he walked sometimes.

My mother chopped the cucumber into thin slices, tossing the rotted parts. "The other two must have caught what she had."

"Doesn't the school keep track of these things?"

"They were sick, Vin. What do you want me to say? Kids stay home when they're sick. Or else they get the other kids sick. And then we'd never hear the end of it."

He kept his eyes on her as he took his seat at the table. "I'll drive you girls to school tomorrow. Make sure you're up." He untwisted a bag of bread rolls.

My mother avoided us as she took a seat, concentrating on the salad bowl in the center of the table.

"Can we get Munchkins?" Sofia asked.

"Sure thing. As long as you wake up the first time I call you."

My mother reached for the pitcher of lemonade grimy with fingerprints, shakily poured it into her glass. Quiet tears rolled from her eyes to her mouth, seeping into the crease between her lips. I lowered my head to my plate, but my eyes kept searching for her. I couldn't look away, couldn't leave her there like that.

"What's wrong?" my father asked in a flat tone.

"Nothing." She swiped at her cheeks, straightened, and for a moment, I thought she was going to pull herself together. Then, after a few seconds: "It wouldn't be this way if you showed your face before nine o'clock at night."

He took a big bite of his bread roll.

"Have to be out gallivanting with your deadbeat friends. Smelling of booze. Your family's your last priority," she said.

"Oh, yeah? Is that why I'm working my ass off?" He took another bite, showing off a wet chew.

"For something that only you want."

"That's not true."

"Your wife doesn't want it."

My father continued to eat.

"Your kids don't want it."

My ears pricked. What was she talking about? None of us had expressed this to her.

"Is that true? You girls don't want to move?" He seemed to be genuinely asking. He sounded hurt.

"It's not true," I said for us, though I wasn't sure what we all wanted, what I wanted.

"Oh, I get it," my mother said. "It's just me who's the last priority."

My father didn't respond and we moved into the meal in silence.

Things will be different," he announced, driving us to school the next morning. The truck jolted as we made our way down the pitted road, unseen objects pinging and shifting. There was a pack of sunflower seeds in the cup holder. A water bottle beside it was filled with spittle and shells. I tried not to look at it. Pinned together in his truck, we half listened to radio sports commentary, passing a box of Munchkins. We lapped at our powdered lips. Sofia was covered in doughnut mess, plucking furiously at her tights. Sugar dust ballooned and curled in the air.

"Everything will be better when we're in the new house," he said, pulling into the lot. "The new school. You'll see. Mom's just going through a difficult time." He reached for me, warming the back of my neck with his hand. He knew I was sensitive. Settling deeper into the seat, I felt his sometimes-cold clumsiness dissolve.

To my right, Sofia stuck her fingers up her jacket sleeve to scratch the crook of her elbow, which was red and bumpy with eczema. She'd had it since she was two years old, unabated, the dry itch soothed only by thick coats of prescription ointment and lukewarm oatmeal baths. My father was paranoid about her unclean fingernails infecting the open wounds. He told me to look out for a single red line leading to Sofia's heart, signifying a blood infection. Sofia's delicacy made me protective of her and also crushingly nervous.

"No scratching," my father said, stretching over me to yank Sofia's hand out of her jacket sleeve. My neck turned cool again.

He leaned hard to the curb. Road maps rushed across the dashboard. He pulled up to the school and gave his knees a few musical slaps. "All set?"

While the other two started collecting their things, I fiddled with the plastic barrette I used to hold my bangs. I pressed the metal against my scalp again and again.

"What's going on with Mom?" I finally asked. Lia and Sofia stopped moving.

"She's . . . being stubborn. She's afraid of change? I don't really know." He eyed the pine tree air freshener as it swung from the rearview mirror. He blinked, massaged his thumb—the one he'd broken as a child and that had never healed the right way. "We just have to show her that we love her, and that we miss her. The new house will cheer her up, I think." I didn't agree with my father. My mother had made it clear she had no interest in moving. I wanted to trust him, though. He blinked again, swiped the bridge of his nose, a nervous habit of his, something he did when he spoke with teachers or other parents, instances when, I suspect, he didn't have much to say.

Beside me, Lia and Sofia quietly argued, both pulling at a keychain on Sofia's backpack. "It's mine," Lia said, trying to pry Sofia's fingers from the glittery dolphin.

"Can we have lunch money?" I asked my father.

"She didn't give you anything?" He shifted in his seat, reaching for his back pocket.

I hadn't meant to betray my mother, but I didn't like the idea of Lia and Sofia picking at stale rice cakes while everyone else ate normal food.

My father pulled a fifty-dollar bill out of his wallet. "Can they break this?"

"Maybe," I said, taking the bill from him. I dreaded having to walk up to the lunch woman who never looked you in the eyes, who always seemed annoyed.

"If she tries to keep you home again, you call me," my father said. "You have the number, right?"

I recited the digits in my head, knowing I wouldn't use them, knowing that my father could never be on call for us during his busy mornings.

"Be the big sister, Anna," he said as we filed out of the truck.

I mumbled an okay, meeting his eyes in a silent pact. I led my sisters to the school's entrance, where decorative cutouts of paper tulips and daisies looked brash against the gray outside.

Behind me, the engine revved and I let out a shaky breath, my days once again filled with an anxiety I couldn't settle. In my ten-year-old mind, I sensed that my father's anger at my mother would inevitably spread to us. After all, weren't we extensions of her? She'd actually named me after herself. Sometimes, after hearing our names called in succession, my body involuntarily twinged.

As I reached the front doors and turned for a last look, I spotted the line of mothers in their vans, with their toothy smiles, waving to their children.

When we were young girls, I think we confused our father. He frowned at our spontaneous pirouettes in the kitchen and our baby talk, the way we clambered onto his lap as if there were not limbs to bruise. He was never affectionate, especially after work, and he often dozed off while listening to our stories. I watched him tighten whenever Sofia burrowed into his belly or Lia tugged at his neck, leaning his head back to evade them. Maybe he'd wanted sons. My sisters learned to save their dances and curtsies for our mother while I stood on the other side of the room, waiting for my father's discomfort to pass, brushing my hair with my fingers.

At the dinner table, he always seemed trapped, eager to bolt. He didn't ever look happy in pictures, cracking a painful-looking smirk. He did this even in the photos where a three-year-old me balanced on his lap in a frilled cotton dress, preparing to blow out birthday candles. He was different from the other men in our neighborhood, never fitting into the role of loud, warm, Italian American patriarch.

Men don't feel as much as women, my mother used to say.

They don't have as much to talk about. I knew this couldn't be true, though my father could be the kind of withdrawn that made people uncomfortable, a shyness that was almost aggressive. And he seemed, to me, embarrassed by sadness. It was something he regarded as a kind of emotional promiscuity. "You're too sensitive" was his favorite thing to say when I ran to him after a fight with my sisters. Still, I kept holding out for a change in him and could sense that he carried some small privacies, deep and abiding. I believed that one day he'd want to share something of himself, to confide in me.

We didn't miss school for a month. Then, like magic, came a week of heavy rainstorms. The river had swollen in the night, drowning the streets and yards, blocking the only route to school. Our cellar filled up to our father's knees. He took refuge in the front parlor, where he could be alone—one place of happy seclusion in a house with three wild girls. He thumped on the walls when we made too much noise, running through the halls in plastic heels or clattering at the table, putting on performances.

My mother was content to be inside, surrounded by her family. She pulled piles of crafts from the basement, lifted her nightgown to her breasts as she waded in the water muck, saving the supplies from the flood. She taught us how to latch-hook and hot-glue, how to sew cotton-stuffed animals from felt. Around the house, the doors bumped because she had the windows open. Sequins and feathers blew to the floor.

She persuaded my father to help with the trickier, more intricate projects, like structuring the walls of a dollhouse he'd been promising to build for months. We marveled at how easily he erected the walls and roof and then, one by one, began applying the shingles. We hovered around him, the four of us smelling like sleep and worn clothes, lazy. We spent the rest of the afternoon painting the miniature window frames white while my father coated the outside walls in a luxurious shade of green. My mother stood behind him, her fingers dancing around his scalp, running through his bed head. She kissed him on the nape of his neck and for the first time in weeks, my father didn't pull away.

Late in the afternoon, my sisters and I retreated to the family room, sprawled on the ragged carpet to watch cartoons. This was the cleanest part of the house, breathable. I'd lie on my back listening to the rain beat outside, drumming on windowsills and trash barrels. Like my mother, I felt protected indoors, by the purring rain, by each other, shoulder to shoulder with my sisters.

Eventually, the rain slackened and stopped, and my mother returned to her bed, where she studied the clear, cloudless blue out the window as if it were an insult. Maybe the sky seemed indifferent to her in its freshness, its continuity; the world spinning on as she willed it not to.

For a long time afterward, my mother talked about that week of rain like it was one of the happiest times of her life. There was nothing so exciting to her as feeling close, cooped up, a little endangered. The five of us against something greater than ourselves.

7

There lives in me the memory of a mother who will not die. A mother I won't forget, no matter how long she's been changed. Her image stays with me in the mornings when I sit on the fire escape, lonely and slumped over tea, watching the dirty breath of the subway curl from the grates. Watching men sweep slush from their storefronts, spreading fistfuls of salt.

There's a creeping urge to dial back the clock, to do something useful. There are friends I've lost touch with. It would be nice to sit across from one of them in a cozy space downtown, to talk about our lives over french fries and cake, admiring the petals of a succulent centerpiece. This is the beginning of my life. Shouldn't I be pursuing something, launching myself into adulthood? I don't feel like I have anything to talk about, three years out of school. It's an effort to wash a cereal bowl, to walk the ten-minute commute to the restaurant where I wait tables. There's a load I carry with me, something I've inherited that pulses when I'm left alone.

Make the call.

I return to my room, shimmy under the sheets, and turn the

medical show back on. But I can't concentrate. There's a woman singing somewhere in the building. Maybe she's standing with her arms outstretched, a calico kitten circling her legs. Her singing allows me to believe for a moment that I am truly living, that this spontaneous splendor is what I originally sought from the city. Somehow, it will transmit from her to me, give some meaning to the hours I've spent lying here, flat on my back, fingering the tuft of black that swells beneath my underwear. I am less alone with the echoes of people out in the world, their voices ringing around.

Vera comes back tonight. She'll want to talk about her trip to Jonathan's as soon as she walks through the door. Maybe I'll pretend to be asleep.

The place is a mess. It's not just my room, which is filled with oatmeal bowls and used Kleenex. The apartment looks bad. I've let the air stale. I light a candle and put it near her side of the couch. Then I pretend-clean the kitchen, dropping empty wine bottles in the trash though they should be recycled. I wipe the gritty counters with water-soaked bath towels, brush coffee grinds into the nook behind the toaster. I don't want Vera to leave our ancient apartment, stained and cluttered with our shared lives. I don't behave in a way that makes a case for her staying.

In the shower, a spider crouches by the shampoo bottle. I keep a watchful eye as its legs twitch and rise, but I don't want to kill it. Eventually, I aim the showerhead and watch it be limply dragged, body first, toward the drain.

∞

By the open window, I read and wait, letting snowflakes spit on my knees. The curtains blow into the room like sails. Downstairs, the door to the building opens and there's a gush of wind up three drafty flights. Footsteps and the jingle of keys. I know the difference between Vera's banging sprint up the steps and the slow trudge of the other tenants. It isn't her.

Back to the window. Now I see her, an overnight duffel bouncing against her hip.

I feel a little cruel as I dart to the bedroom and close the door. Vera comes into the apartment and drops her keys on the counter. Her shoes block the light beneath my door as she hesitates in the hall. My room is dark. It wouldn't be unlike her to open the door anyway, to flick on the lights and rock me awake. "No sleeping," she might say. "I haven't seen you in days!"

She drops her bag in the hall and goes back to the kitchen, singing to herself. She unscrews a wine bottle and fills a glass. I stay in bed, listening, barely breathing under the covers.

I am not my mother.

Without giving myself time to think, I roll out of bed and push my door open.

"I thought you were sleeping," she says, poking her head around the corner. "Come hang with me!" Vera is glowing. She can't seem to stop smiling and I immediately regret coming to see her. She does a little booty shake before entering her room, some wine slipping from her glass and onto the doorframe. She unzips her suitcase. She always unpacks the second she arrives home.

Idling in her doorway, I stretch and fake yawn. "You had a good time?" I ask.

She pauses midfold, a dopey look on her face. "It was amazing."

"Aw. Good," I say. I can't take it. "Let's catch up tomorrow."

I am not my mother. I am not. I am not.

Sunday morning, the neighbors are on the balcony again. I open my window to hear them more clearly, to feel accompanied. After a few moments of listening, I slip both hands down my underwear. It's hard to come while concentrating on their words. Can they hear me through the window—the back of my hand chafing cotton? Can they see the shadow of my open legs on the wall? I move fast, locking my breath, imagining they can hear. I move until my fingers ache, until it's almost too much to bear. Every limb is humming, pressed into the sheets.

When I head out for a coffee, Vera notices me sneaking past her room. "Where are you going?" she calls from her bed, voice coated in sleep. Her door is always open.

"Just for a walk."

"Grab me a coffee?" she asks. "Medium iced? No sugar?" Her hair is frizzed and wild. Her breasts are exposed, one nipple protruding more than the other. She makes no attempt to cover up, never has. Vera's lack of inhibition, her ease in her own body and refusal to conceal it, is something I find comforting; a permission that I could also be this way, if I wanted. As she lets out one of her gross morning coughs—too many cigarettes—I realize how happy I am to have her back.

"You want a chocolate cruller with that, Marky?" I ask, dialing up the Boston accent.

She responds in kind. "That's wicked nice of you, Darlene."

"You got it." I pause before slipping out. "I can wait if you want to come?"

"You sure you don't mind?" The way she says this—with such surprise and sincerity. I've become rough, impatient, someone who makes others cautious.

She grabs a sweater and a pair of jeans from the floor, pulls them on without underwear. "Just have to brush my teeth," she says. "Actually, no." She runs her tongue over them. "Actually, I probably should."

We both laugh, and I'm feeling pleased with myself. Like I've done the right thing.

We walk to a Riverside bench with coffees and bagels. Vera rips her bagel apart and a lump of cream cheese falls onto her scarf. She gathers it up with a finger, swipes it on her tongue. I can tell she's in a good mood by the way she bounces, stuffing her mouth. "Sorry," she says. "I know I'm being gross."

I let out a short laugh. Half of me is far away, replaying Lia's voicemail. The other is trying to navigate the best way to tell Vera. My breath is thinning. I have to unzip my coat.

"I'm really happy I went," she says abruptly, picking seeds off her lap. "It was so much fun."

"Good!" I tell her, in the most genuine way I can muster. "What are his parents like?"

"They're sweet. Different. Very religious."

"Like, pray-before-dinner religious?"

"No, but. Lots of crosses and Marys around the house. I could tell his mom was happy to have a girl around."

"I'm glad you had fun," I say, asking more questions about the meals they ate and the films they watched. I try my best to seem engaged, to not steer attention from her happiness.

Something changes though. Vera leans back on the bench to stretch. It seems like she's stalling. She pulls at her sleeves in a nervy way. "Actually. I have news."

It hadn't crossed my mind before, but suddenly I know what's coming. Vera knows that I know. I take a huge bite of my bagel to hide my face.

"Jonathan asked me to move in with him."

"What did you say?" It's all I can manage.

She's wearing this shy expression that's unlike her.

"When do you think you'll move out?" I rip a small piece of bagel but don't eat it.

"I know it seems so fast." She's talking, her mouth is moving. I can only think about what's going to happen to me. "I really do love him. I've never felt like this about anyone."

"Love?" When did that happen?

"We've been saying it for a couple of weeks. I know it seems crazy. But it feels right."

"You were just talking about texting the married guy," I say.

"I was drunk, feeling mischievous." She gives me a knowing look. "What, you want me to go after Married Guy now?"

"No, obviously not."

"It feels really, really right," she keeps saying.

"Yeah, sure," I say, throwing a piece of bagel to a squirrel. "If you know, you know."

"I'll help you with finding a subletter and all that. I won't leave you stranded," she says, laying her hands dramatically on my lap.

"No, yeah." I wave her off. "Of course."

"And you know you're coming over every Thursday for movie night."

She watches me tear off another piece and throw it to the squirrel, who's been joined by a friend.

Beautiful Vera with her mud-blond curls, her sparkling green eyes. The contagious laugh that sounds as if there's a swig of milk caught in her throat. I can see right through her. But she can see right through me, can summon my past in an instant. With so many years behind us, we can use our shared background as a weapon against each other. There's a watchful attitude. Territorial. As if both of us are thinking the same thing: *I know who you really are.*

"I'm happy for you, Vera. You deserve a good guy for once." I think I mean it. I don't want to spoil this moment.

"Thank you." She crumples her bagel bag. "I'll stop talking about myself. Tell me about your weekend." She digs a cigarette out of her pocket and lights it, takes a long drag and swings both legs onto the bench, curling them beneath her, signaling she's ready to listen.

"No, no. Keep going," I say. "Your life is more interesting."

She elbows me. "You're sad. Did some shithead hurt your feelings? Tell me who to beat up."

"I'm fine," I say, making an attempt at laughter. "I promise."

"I know when something's bothering you, Anna. I've known you since you were twelve."

That's right, I want to say. *And now you're leaving me.*

When I look back at Vera, there's a splotch of cream cheese on her nose. She's keeping a straight face. Somehow, despite my despairing mood, it's the funniest thing I've ever seen, and I'm touched that she knows I need cheering up. I wipe it off with a napkin, laughing.

"Come on," she says.

I can't get anything past her.

"Talk to me."

"It's nothing. I just—I got a weird call from Lia. A voicemail. I'm too scared to call back. I know it's about my mom."

"Oh, man. What did the message say?"

"She wants me to call her back. But she was so frantic. Not herself."

"You haven't called? When was this?"

"Two days ago? Friday night."

"You need to call her, Anna. It could be serious."

"I don't want to go back there. I really don't. No one can stand me anyway. We'll just fight."

"Maybe you don't have to go back, but you have to at least call. Anna." She gives me a knowing look, a look that tells me I'm being selfish, making excuses.

I last saw my sisters four months ago, when they came to New York with my father. Sofia was thoughtful, bringing a list of trendy dessert shops and pop-up stores she wanted to visit. She gave me an update on her boyfriend, Dylan, the gifts he'd gotten her, the surprise dates. I felt giddy myself, knowing she deserved it. There's something about Sofia—sweeter each time I see her. She tried to tidy my room the last time, brought me a vase of flowers. Lia sat silent at every restaurant, chiming in only when Sofia or my father tried to lessen the strain with a question. I could call Sofia, but then there'd be no way out of going home.

"Don't you think Lia would have called again?" I ask. "Or even texted you? It can't be that bad."

"She's probably being just as stubborn as you. You need to make the move." She puts her hand over mine.

"I will. I will," I say, pulling my hand away to scratch it, though it doesn't itch.

8

With my mother sedated and sleeping away the day, I snuck into her room. I ran my hands over her long wooden dresser, the color of molasses, moistened and swollen from the open windows. Every drawer was packed with musty clothes she'd stopped wearing. On the table-top sat compact powders and uncapped nail polish bottles, dried out and useless.

I knew of no cure for her sadness except to speak ill of my father. Or maybe to stay in Everett. Whatever the solution. I knew we girls were no longer enough. She needed someone to take care of her, someone who listened. She now wept openly for her own mother, a grief that she'd usually kept to herself. It seemed to have worsened, spilling out for anyone to witness, the unwanted move heightening emotions she'd long ignored.

Nonna died when my mother was around seven years old. Living close to her childhood home, I think, was a constant re-minder of Nonna. There was the cinema where they used to sneak candy in Nonna's purse, and the drugstore where they sat upon old-fashioned stools to sip lime rickeys. My mother pointed these things out to us, rarely speaking in detail, instead nibbling her bottom lip, rapidly changing the subject.

Her reserve gave me space to dream. I'd only seen a picture of Nonna once or twice. I imagined her in headscarves, gorgeous, oceanic blues and greens, the graceful ripple of her shoulder blades, like wings. Or my mother as a girl, sitting by Nonna's hospital bed, lifting a cardboard straw to her gray lips. Maybe she kissed her forehead to say goodbye. This was vague, invented. Without a real story to cling to, it felt to me like my grandmother was not dead but still dying somewhere. I didn't know how she died, only that she was no longer here.

I found it odd that no one talked about her, not even the neighbors. My mother ignored us whenever we said Nonna's name aloud—unless of course she was drinking or in some dreamily cheery mood, and then she'd ramble on about the happier times, memories like their movie theater adventures.

One night in May, we heard her crooning our names from the upstairs bath, where we found her crying in the tub. My sisters and I circled her on the cold tile, our nightgowns clear and wet, clinging to our skin. I studied the dusting of freckles on her shoulders and in the concave of her breasts. We looked nothing like her with our olive skin and pitch-black hair, the three of us clones of our father.

We wrapped bath towels around our legs, dipped our skinny arms over the edge to soak them in the water. We were careful not to elbow the glass bottles of cleansing oils that lined the lip of the tub. It was a claustrophobic space, but one I wanted to linger in, the steady drip of the faucet pulling me into almost sleep.

Meanwhile, my father was in Cambridge, eating veal and rapini, careening down cobblestoned streets with cigars and whiskey on his breath. That's what my mother told us. He'd been promoted from construction laborer to project manager for the new development we were moving into, retiring the hard hat and blue jeans for a suit and tie. As a result, he had to spend late evenings with potential clients, wealthy real estate developers and agents, entertaining them with dinners and drinks. He claimed he didn't want to be out all those hours. He had to keep up appearances and forge new relationships. My mother chided him for being a lightweight, unable to keep pace with the others. When he came home tipsy, crawling up the stairs, she'd say, "Three drinks and you're slurring like a three-year-old." Our father's absence was the price we were paying for a new home, the only way we could afford it. He was responsible for sectioning off the land and transforming it into lots, putting in roads, sewers, and utilities, getting the houses built.

She'd called us to the bathroom to turn us against him.

"Tell him you don't want to move," she said, though it was definitely happening, only a couple of months away. "He'll listen to you." It wasn't clear if she was talking to me or to all of us at once. There was desperation in her voice—a weakness I detested. She was helplessly, contagiously sad, her nutmeg hair twisted in a cluster atop her head, her face eternally half asleep. I feared she wouldn't come with us to the new house, that I would have to make a choice between my parents.

In the tub, she tilted her head so that she kissed her own shoulder. She held a washcloth against her mouth, dragged it across her lips until they raised and blurred at the edges, the skin around them scoured and raw.

"I'm not moving if you aren't," Lia said to my mother, her glasses fogged from the steam.

Sofia nodded, seeming less sure than Lia.

My mother ducked her head under the faucet to slurp from the stream of warm water. "If you had to choose," she said, raising her head, "who would you pick?"

"You," Lia said with confidence, swiping her lenses with two fingers.

My mother reached her arm across the tub, hurling water out the sides. She gripped Lia's chin and pinched it, a white spot blooming where her fingers had been. "Good girl," she said. "You love your mother."

I felt accused. She was testing us, challenging our loyalty to her. I feigned ignorance, her demands making me feel split and restless. My mother. Ruthless and scheming, dispersing her sick love. There was a part of me, and I think a part of my sisters, that aspired to give her that alliance, believing it would make her come back to us.

"I pick you too!" Sofia chimed, reaching for the bowl of bath beads. She loved to prick and pop them with her nails.

My mother narrowed her eyes at me. Did she think I would never be able to love her enough? "Who knows what Anna would do," she said, unsmiling. She could sense my shifting allegiance to the other parent, the one I could trust. Late at night, I made tallies, trying to decide which one of them I'd be better off without. Had she learned to read my mind?

My chest tightened when she leaned closer, close enough that I could smell her sour breath. Rough patches had dried on her cheeks, blushed with rosacea. Her red hair, half wet and coiling, made the bumps stand out even more. *You're ugly*, I thought, withdrawing. *Ugly.*

"Who's here with you now?" she hissed. "Who's with you every day?" She snatched my arm. "Answer me." Her nails dug in, and I thought she might tear away a piece of me.

"You are," I breathed.

"And who's not?"

"Dad."

"That's right. The friggin' degenerate."

I ignored the pain in my arm to lock my eyes with hers. She was smirking. The water sloshed when my mother drew back in the tub, leaning against the edge so her breasts were in full view. Slack and floating, browned nipples crinkled.

"I know," she said, to all of us. "She'd pick her mother."

On the windowsill, a pile of chalky tablets next to an open pill bottle disintegrated in a puddle of grime. *Eat them*, I thought. *So that you fall asleep. So that we don't have to listen to you.* I couldn't keep track of the pills anymore, the different sizes and shapes. I couldn't tell what they were for.

When she finished her bath, my sisters swirled the filmy water. My mother rose slowly from the tub, revealing the ripples of her stomach and the wiry pubic hair below. Her legs were unshaven. Spider veins like the cracks in porcelain.

Eventually, at dusk, she emerged from her spell. She scooped dollops of ricotta cheese and honey on toast, set napkins and placemats on the table. Briefly, my mother was joyful, basking in the falseness of our happy quartet. We scooped pistachio ice cream from the tub until our tongues went numb. While we ate, she finger-combed her hair, raking through the wet knots, her arms wobbling, skin sagging from her bones like hung clothes.

All around us, the blackened windows reflected the lighted rooms of our house, eclipsing the outside world. I avoided our reflections; the distorted, faceless figures seated at the table, disturbed by the way we morphed into sameness. I didn't want to be related to this creature, this imposter who'd come to stay.

I focused on the Italian farm-girl figurines that sat on the shelf behind my mother—their glassy faces gleaming beneath the yellow light, their bodies swimming in skirts that drowned their feet. My sisters and I liked to point out our favorites. Mine was the girl in the lilac skirt, a gray, stringy-haired puppy propped in her wicker basket.

I was pulled away from this when I noticed my mother beginning to fade, her head bobbing, eyes growing heavy. She tongued the cold spoon until green dripped from her lips and chin. She dug in for more, but opened her mouth too early, when the ice cream was still inches from her tongue.

I didn't know it then, but she was high. She burrowed for

something in her pocket, popped two or three orange pills in her mouth. It looked like she was eating little bugs. Her head lolled when the drugs took over, her words becoming elongated, warped. Soon, she was asleep. This gave me an aching feeling in my stomach, a feeling of worry. At least she looked peaceful, gentle.

I draped a fleece over her shoulders and left her sleeping at the table, led my sisters upstairs where the three of us lay snug-tight in one bed. We craved the comfort of proximity—warm bubble-gum breath hitting cheeks, soft legs brushing. My sisters grew motionless beside me and I resisted drifting off, lulled by their sleeping sounds. I envisioned seeing us from above, a tangled unit. The image brought me comfort. I reeled on the cusp of unconsciousness, clinging to the temporary calm, the warm stillness. I was aware that it could vanish at any moment.

Of the three of us, Lia was quickest to please our mother. She responded to her capriciousness with self-reliance rather than retreat. I don't know where this bravery came from. She was usually treated the worst—a clue that something in my mother had been on the verge of cutting loose.

I remembered years earlier, Lia being six or seven, driving my mother crazy. I was in the front parlor playing house with Sofia, when I heard them yelling in the bedroom. I crept in the doorway to spy, picking at the peeling paint on the wall.

"Lia is going to her new parents," my mother said when she spotted me. She turned back to my sister. "They're coming. Your new family. I just called them." She started riffling through our drawers, pulling out watermelon-print shorts and then a smiley-face T-shirt stained with sauce, shoving them into the suitcase.

Lia tugged on my mother's robe. "If I'm good, can I come back?" she asked in a shaky voice.

"You've had enough chances."

Lia frowned and sniffled. She went to the corner of the room, reached inside her pink wicker basket and pulled out some Polly Pockets. "Can I bring a toy?" she asked, waving the plastic cases in the air so they clicked open, revealing their miniature worlds. A few of the people fell to the floor. She crouched and shuffled them into a neat pile, scooped them up.

When my mother didn't respond, I thought she had come to her senses. Then she zipped up the suitcase, took Lia by the arm and yanked her through the house as I ran after them, until she thrust Lia onto the front steps. Lia used two hands to pull her suitcase over the threshold.

"They'll be here any minute," my mother said.

Lia gently pushed on the screen door, opening it just a little, and my mother snapped it closed with her palm. "Nope."

Lia tried again.

"Nope."

"Stop it," I choked out, kneading a bony fist into my mother's side. "Let her in." I tried to open the door but my mother threw her palm at me, forcing me to the wall. My elbow knocked against the wood and I cried out at the white-hot pain.

"Oh, cut it out," she said to me. "It didn't hurt." I could tell by the flush in her cheeks and ears she was worried she'd gone too far. She crossed her arms and scanned the street.

My sister was quiet, her eyes wet with tears, her little pink suitcase by her side.

All the while, Sofia watched the scene from the middle of the hall. She sat on her knees, her nose running, flyaway hairs clinging to her forehead.

9

Sunday night, Broadway Tavern is blaring with generic Americana—twanging, high-pitched voices that grate. I'm ready to make money, to live the next six hours in a blur. I'm scrounging the side station for pens when I feel a buzzing in my apron's front pocket. It's my father's name on the screen. Without checking to see who's watching, I hurry to the bathroom, the one that's meant for customers. I lock myself in the last stall, hands shaking as the ringing fades out. He leaves a voicemail.

"Hon? Are you getting our calls?" A shaky pause. "Come on, Anna. Don't do this to me. Call back." He is usually calm and certain, in control. Now, he is close to tears.

There's something about hearing my father in pain. It breaks me. I picture him on the other end of the line, sitting in his home office. He's wearing a beanie and sweatshirt, thick socks because the heat doesn't reach that part of the house.

It's not that I don't love my father, that I don't want to teleport through the phone right then to be there for him. It's that I don't know if I can handle what he has to say. And I think they might be better off without me. I know deep down that I've lost control of my emotions, that I overspeak, that I sometimes don't know when I've breached a person's limit. I feel an increasing need to get my point across, even if it hurts. I don't trust myself in a room with my mother. They're better off without me. All of them.

When I scramble from the stall, my manager, Martina, is standing outside of it with her arms crossed. "Seriously, Anna."

"Sorry," I automatically say, caught with the phone in my hand. "It won't happen again."

Back on the floor, the tables have filled for the big game. It's only minutes before the servers are running around, our faces polished with sweat. We're waiting for clean silverware, and the water pitchers need to be refilled. The side bar is piling with drinks I should be running. My sloppiness isn't going unnoticed. From behind the bar, Roxanne is giving me the eyes. *What on earth are you doing?* I've been at Broadway for two years. I'm dependable, hardworking. I make the most tips. I'm the one people turn to when they're drowning. Today, I can't read my own handwriting. I've typed in the wrong order twice.

"Are you okay?" asks Tal, my closest work friend. "What's going on?"

I look left and right, not sure where her voice is coming from.

She puts both hands on my arms, twirls me around. "Tell me. What do you need?"

"Can you check on the silverware? That five-top doesn't have any knives and their food's about to come up."

"Yes. Go take care of those drinks." She points to the side bar with her chin. When I start to walk away, Tal tugs me back. "Actually, wait."

Oh, no. "What?"

"That guy looks pissed. Take care of that before Martina sees."

It's one of my tables, an older man in a button-down. He sits straight with importance, a pile of papers next to his crossed arms. A Columbia professor, no doubt. I forgot to put in his order. A bacon burger with sweet potato fries. He shakes his head as I make my way over. He's almost smiling, excited to berate me. "I've been sitting here for over an hour."

"I'm sorry—"

"Forget it. I'm leaving. And I'm not paying for that," he says, pointing to his three-dollar iced tea. He leaves. Fortunately, Martina doesn't notice.

The pace of a crowded restaurant usually excites and distracts. It's not working tonight. When I close out at one o'clock, my legs are shaking and I can't feel my feet. I collapse in the last stall, smelling myself. My father's voice haunting. *Don't do this to me.* I picture a life without either of my parents, how lost I would be. I keep picturing them dead. It's too quiet in here. Too quiet at home. If I lie in bed, I won't be able to sleep.

There are some regulars at the bar. I could join them, though it's frowned upon after a shift to let customers see you drinking. Maybe if I have just one. I dab my underarms with soapy paper towels, smooth my eyebrows and rustle my hair. I get back out there.

In the early hours of morning, the men turn their backs to me, becoming lost in military drama. I find myself slipping off the stool clumsily, not saying goodbye. It's my favorite time of night. All the bars are closed, but secretly open to local waitstaff. I can hear the row of clandestine parties, can see shapes through the fogged windows, laughing, basking in their intimate little worlds.

I must be drunk because my fingers are purpled, gloveless, but I can't feel a thing. There's a ringing in my ears. Ahead of me is the blue *Laundromat* sign, signaling the turn home. I speed up, and that's when I notice Lawrence walking in my direction, jingling his keys. When he doesn't immediately notice me, I step in the middle of the sidewalk, expecting, laughing in a flirting way.

"Look who it is," he says. He opens his arms and I bounce into them, letting him rock me in the cold. The wool of his coat is warm but the silver buttons are like icicles against my cheek. He reeks of cigarettes. "You just get off your shift?" he asks, pushing me away, taking me in with his gaze.

"Kind of." I brush my hair back self-consciously.

"Ah. Wait a minute." He leans closer, inspecting. "Just got off the barstool?"

I stick out my tongue and close my eyes, staggering a little. "I'm supposed to be heading home." I stumble through the words.

"But I'm wide awake." I don't know if I'm this drunk or if I'm only pretending to be, dumbing myself down because he'll think it's cute.

"I was going to meet the guys, but you can come back to mine if you want?" He steps aside, offering me his arm. We walk the few blocks to his apartment, passing mine on the way.

I've known Lawrence for two years. He thinks it's hot to fuck me on the table where his roommates leave their cereal spoons. Afterward, I go home and stand in the blazing shower until my skin begins to itch. I stare in the mirror, at the knob of my tail-bone bruised mucky blue.

Before Jonathan came into our lives, Vera and I spent most of our time at the pub around the corner, fishing for Lawrence's attention. He wore tight T-shirts to show off his arms, the taut muscles of his neck and shoulders. There was something tattooed on his right biceps, a vase or a bowl filled with fruit. It was an unspoken rivalry, waiting for him to favor one of us over the other: a free drink, a wink, some conversation. Of course, he wanted either of us, neither of us, both of us at once.

"Let me guess," he said one night, leaning toward Vera and me. He rested his elbows on the damp wooden bar top. Sometimes, he touched us, stroking the sides of our necks or cupping our cheeks, like little kittens. We both agreed we would never hook up with him because something about him was "off."

"You're the happy one," he said, pointing at Vera. "And you're the sad one."

"Excuse me?" I said, in a moment of defiance, but we knew it was true. If it weren't for Vera's incessant, over-the-top happiness, I wouldn't have to balance us out with my gloom.

"She doesn't like when people say stuff like that," said Vera, sipping from her straw.

"You just—you have those Bambi eyes," said Lawrence.

"I don't even know what that means," I said,

"You're not being nice," Vera told him, trying to defend me but still playing, still smiling.

He reached his hand toward my cheek and I pulled away. "Relax," he said. "It was meant to be a compliment."

We'd been there for an hour, two whiskey sodas in, when Vera announced she was leaving me to meet Jonathan in Chinatown. It was early on a Saturday evening, no later than eight o'clock, and I didn't want to go back to our apartment by myself. Neither of us had ever been alone with the bartender.

This is how I remember it: Vera kissed me on the cheek and sailed out the door, and to make myself feel less abandoned, I stayed fastened to that stool until close, watching Lawrence clean glasses and count cash while he poured me drink after drink. In a whiskey haze, I allowed him to walk me home and come up to use the toilet. Before I knew it we were fucking on the couch with most of our clothes on, his hands gripping my neck for real, until I was coughing, pleading with my Bambi eyes for him to stop. I made him leave after that because I didn't want to wake up to his face, thought maybe if he wasn't there in the morning it'd be like it never happened. I didn't tell Vera. When I suggested we try a different bar, she didn't question it, but I caught her more than once, looking over my shoulder to read our texts.

It makes me feel hollow, scooped out, but I keep going to him. Sometimes it's better just to feel something.

The next night, on Monday, I meet an old classmate who lives across town, on East Ninety-Eighth. With him, too, I'm downing shots of whiskey, talking without intimacy. I'm trying to ignore the stubby fingers wrapped around his glass, nails chewed to the quick. We sit with our knees bent uncomfortably under his coffee table, and my head's spinning by the time he's carrying me like a bride to his room, tossing me on the flannel sheets. He falls in love with his own seducing, kissing me through my underwear for too long. In the middle of the night, he swings a leg over my abdomen, like I'm a pile of pillows. When he starts to snore, I slip away, taking the subway card stashed on the table by the door.

On Tuesday, while Vera's at work, I go through her things. I sit on the white sheets among her moonstones and dried flowers, the gorgeous, expensive makeup set assembled on her bureau. I sink into the bed, pretending the room and these objects are mine. Perfume bottles that glisten in the cut of diagonal sunlight, a closet so full of clothes the door won't shut. On the built-in shelves sit figurines from trips to Europe with her mother— Gaudí-inspired elephant statues, blown glass from Venice. In the mirror, I apply Vera's lipstick with a steady hand, a bright pink that doesn't match my olive skin. I run her comb through my hair. I spray her perfume, bergamot and jasmine, ignoring the packing boxes leaning against the wall, waiting to be filled.

It's cold but I'm steaming by the time I've walked the thirty-ish blocks to meet her for happy hour. Sweat gathers beneath my breasts and behind my ears, at the base of my spine.

Cast in the neon lights of the bar, Vera is mesmerizing. Her lips are a matte pink, like petals against her dewy complexion—the color works for her. The dress code at the marketing firm is casual, but she looks extravagant every day, wearing jewel-tone fabrics that sheen and brighten her green eyes.

I wonder if she can tell that I'm wearing her lipstick, if she can smell herself on my wrists. If she does notice, she's not letting it show. Vera carries the same grace with her as she did when she was a girl, smiling at nothing, absently fingering her gold hoop earrings, seeing what you want her to see and being okay with it. An elegance I used to cherish.

The truth is, envy strikes me every time Vera speaks, at every declaration of a new diet or exercise regimen, her will to better herself in general, her ambition to make new friends, her giddiness over Jonathan. I want to be like her, and I don't. Being near her reminds me of my family.

I take a sip of the beer she has waiting for me and she compliments my rings, two or three stacked on each finger. I'm imitating her style, she must know this, but her praise seems genuine. Vera grips my forearm, bends close, so that I can feel her breath on my face. "I'm glad you came out," she says, looking at me for a few extra beats, showing she means it.

To wash away my father, I drink. I finish my beer and I order another, and another. I like the name, Delirium, and the little pink elephant on the label. I sip it down, eyeing the bartender as he empties a shaker, willing him to look back at me. I give Vera vague responses to whatever she's saying. I've forgotten how to feign interest in other people's lives. Vera's especially. The way she goes on and on.

Lia would tell me that I'm being too sensitive—that I need to learn how to hide my feelings about Jonathan. She predicted that this would happen, that Vera and I were too close to live together. It would only ruin our friendship. "You're going to start fights," is what she said to me. "Like you always do."

Lia's voice replays in my mind, urging me to call. I hope Vera doesn't ask if I have. Another part of me wants her to ask, to heave me out of the bar this instant and bring me home to Boston.

She's telling one of her stories about a crazy coworker, when she catches me daydreaming, staring above her shoulder. "Anna," she says, insulted. "What are you looking at?"

"Sorry."

"Should we get out of here?"

When our boots hit the sidewalk, she loops her arm in mine, throws half of her scarf around my shoulders. I'm excited for the two of us to slather on our clay masks and snuggle together in our oversized robes, maybe doze off to a movie. No talking, just being next to each other.

"Should we stop by Gristedes?" I ask. "Pick out some snacks? Cheez-Its!"

"I wish. I told Jonathan he could come over tonight. We were going to watch a movie."

I let my arm go slack in hers.

"You can watch with us," she says, trying to get close again.

"That's okay. I don't want to intrude."

That same night, my phone flashes a message. *Hey Mouse, you free?*

I met him on a dating app. He calls me Mouse because of the way I burrow into him. I call him He because his name isn't saved in my phone—because for the past few weeks, he's only texted me to come over after eleven. He's one of the new many, a series of no-names.

Funny, the sides of themselves these men tend to unveil to me, cast in shadows. The defenseless groans, mouth gaping, eyes wrinkled shut. The hands reaching for my throat. I consider going over there, but don't have the energy to wash, to get dressed.

Later, when Vera's having sex, I watch the shadows of branches that fan my bedroom floor. Rain pelts with fury. I listen to the swish of Vera's sheets, the anticipation, her pleading whimpers. I fall asleep thinking of him holding her, blowing breaths onto her neck, fingers light across her back. Thinking of their closeness, I wait patiently for the morning my life begins.

10

By June, moving day was around the corner. The boxes meant for packing were still unfolded, stacked against walls, and near to toppling. Closets and cabinets burst with junk while our mother traipsed around in a daze. I suspected things would stay that way until the moving van pulled up.

Lia, Sofia, and I sat on the front porch one afternoon, shoveling a gallon bucket of Richie's Italian ice. Spoons clashed as we battled it out. We worked on the slush until our molars ached, pink juice spraying our arms. Finished, we sat bloated with our legs slotted through the railings, mouths numbed and inked red, skin gluing. We could see the air buckling above the pavement.

Our heads shot up when Debbie arrived in the tiny driveway, bearing trash bags and packing tape in her ex-husband's pickup. Days earlier, I'd heard my mother on the phone with her, hostile and abrupt, flat-out lying about what we'd been up to—like Lia and me being busy with piano though we'd been absent from lessons for weeks. I heard her turn down dinner with Debbie, claiming she and my father were cooking homemade gnocchi and meatballs—something we only did when everyone was getting along.

I licked my fingers, watching Debbie as she gathered packing supplies with takeaway burgers and fries pinched beneath her underarms. I was shy when I first saw a person, no matter how well I knew them. She wore a wrinkled band T-shirt and a pair of jeans she'd chopped into shorts. The pits of her T-shirt were tinged yellow.

We followed her inside, where she dumped everything onto the kitchen counter. We eyed the bags of food, warm and stuffed. I was mesmerized by Debbie, by her gold-spun hair and the coral ring on her middle finger, her only extravagance. I wished I were hers.

We first met Debbie when she moved into the house at the end of the block, not long after her divorce. I was four or five at the time. Each day, before Debbie went to work at the local florist, she and my mother met at the Dunkin' Donuts to spend entire mornings dipping chocolate crullers in creamy coffees while they gossiped about neighbors and family dramas. Sometimes, Debbie skipped work entirely. They'd sit with the rest of the midafternooners, who were clad in their Patriots sweatshirts, gold hoop earrings, and acrylic nails—their coffee lids stamped with cranberry lipstick. They were an odd pair: Debbie with her tacky sweaters and my mother with her dark fabrics, hung loose on her shoulders, handmade capes and scarves, like a pretty witch. I tagged along on weekend afternoons, slumped low in the metal seat and spiraling a straw wrapper around my fingers, hoping to overhear something I shouldn't.

Debbie didn't have children of her own. She often drove all of us—my mother included—on errands like trips to Staples when school started, or dentist appointments every six months. She took us to the mall and the beach, anywhere that required the highway because of our mother's fear of driving. Sometimes, Debbie drove us to the movies. She and my mother jammed their pocketbooks with cheap candies from the corner store. Before we hopped out of the car, they poured a big splash of Baileys in their iced coffees and capped the lid.

On our way home, Debbie blasted her favorite CD so loudly the speakers vibrated against our bodies. She half closed her eyes in a dramatic melancholy while we sang along to "Space Oddity," using our fists as microphones, half singing the words. We did this often, a ritual, but I was always surprised when we reached the end of the song.

My father said Debbie was a busybody, a know-it-all—riling my mother up to complain about an undeserved grade we'd received at school, or poor service at a restaurant. One time, she got into a fight with the cashier at the shoe store because my mother wanted to return a pair of flats she'd worn outdoors. The cashier didn't audibly respond, but shook her head with pursed lips. "Use your words," Debbie shouted, jabbing at the counter with her finger. Then she chucked the shoebox at the woman.

During the summer, Debbie joined us at the public pool.

I stayed on the deck with the adults, sipping on virgin margaritas from a thermos while my sisters played mermaids. Salt-and-vinegar chips burned the corners of my mouth because I had to prove I had the taste for them.

On one of those balmy afternoons, when I was eight or nine and my mother had gone home to feed the dog, I did something I had never done—so out of character that even my sisters looked on in suspicion, bobbing in the water, their sticklike arms adorned with fluorescent-pink floaties. Debbie and I were alone on the deck. She was on the ratty green-and-white lawn chair, pale legs spread out on the recliner as she applied sunscreen to her arms and stomach. She leaned back to nap.

Something about her aged, sun-warmed skin made me yearn for her, maybe because I had never seen my own mother rest in the open like that; scarcely dressed, self-assured. I crawled onto the lawn chair with Debbie, nestling against her. She was slow to wrap an arm around my shoulder and give me a squeeze. I could feel her heart thrumming, the blue, protruding veins of her arms taut with tension, and immediately I knew she didn't want me this close. I concentrated on her blond arm hairs, jeweled with pool water from my sisters' splashing. I remained there for another painful moment, counting in my head to five or ten, then I stood and jumped in the freezing pool. When I emerged to the surface, my sisters and Debbie were staring at me.

My mother refused to acknowledge Debbie or the packing materials that afternoon, instead scribbling on her paper napkin. I couldn't see what she was drawing, but I could guess. She liked to sketch pumpkins, acorns, and dandelions. Our names scrawled in half cursive, over and over, like a tic. They appeared on almost every page of her magazines, letters in blue ink, *Anna, Lia, Sofia.* Maybe she thought her written chants would keep us safe. We found our names everywhere—on scrap papers and the backs of envelopes, in the margins of Stop & Shop receipts, stowed away in junk drawers and littered nightstands.

"Morning, Dee." Debbie sat an iced coffee in front of her.

My mother slurped from the straw with pleasure, but didn't say a word.

Debbie must have been used to my mother's unpredictable moods, which now descended without a moment's notice. She stalked over to my sisters, took Lia's glasses off, and rubbed them on her shirt. When she stuck them back on, Lia tipped on her heels from the force. Next she turned to Sofia, smelling an oily strand of her hair and making a face of disgust. There was dandruff sprinkled like salt atop Sofia's head. That was the week Sofia didn't shower, because no one had told her to. A brown splotch of dirt had arrived on her neck like a new birthmark. I caught a whiff of her one evening when she plopped next to me on the couch, light and airy with her little bird bones. "You stink!" I shoved her to the other end and she tumbled to the floor, laughing.

"Look at you three," Debbie said, taking us in. "Ragamuffins." Her tone was light, but her eyes sharp.

Minutes later, she had us on the floor, wrapping plates and glasses with scarves. We devoured the fries she had brought us, two, three, five at a time. Meanwhile, my mother painted the napkins with nail polish, outlining vines and flowers in amethyst pink.

"You feeding these girls, Dee?" Debbie asked, failing to make it sound like a joke, while she cleaned. The sink was clogged, filled to the top with dark, still water. Bits of rice and oatmeal floated on the top. I'd seen Debbie clock it and back off, too disgusted to dip her hand inside the murk.

"You have to get a handle on things," she said, using two hands to drag a loaded trash bag across the kitchen tile. "Should have been packing weeks ago," she added.

She tugged open a cabinet and our school projects avalanched onto the floor—crumpled paper pilgrim hats, jungle animals sculpted from clay. She opened drawers, eyeing the capless pens and board games, tutting. "How do you play Monopoly without the money?" She ripped a pile of gold-starred worksheets and shoved them in the bag.

Lia and I waited for our mother to respond while Sofia, oblivious, sucked ketchup from a little takeout pouch. Some of it got on her arm and she licked all the way up, wrist to elbow.

Debbie saw and said, "These kids are filthy."

Her words hung in the air.

Then came a low voice, rusty from silence. "Excuse me?" my mother said.

All of her was facing Debbie. Her face was red. "What the hell would you know about being a mother?" she said, clutching her robe because she was naked underneath.

Debbie blinked. As far as I knew, she'd never spoken of the

reason she didn't have children. She looked for a moment like she wanted to tear into my mother, inflict more hurt. But she kept quiet; my mother was in too pitiful a place for Debbie to retaliate.

"Aw, what do you want me to say, Debbie? You stand there running your friggin' mouth."

Pink blotches flowered on Debbie's cheeks, down to her neck. "I hope to God you just had a stroke or something," she said.

"Nope." My mother rolled her gaze to the ceiling, appearing to consider it. "Think I'm okay." She ran her palms over a clean napkin, resumed painting.

"You don't talk that way to me. To a friend. Who's just here to help."

"No one asked you to come over. You're *imposing*."

Debbie let the bag slink to the floor, spilling debris. She kicked the pile and marched to the hall, swiveling around before she reached the threshold.

"I'm sorry, girls." She gave us a quick wave. "Get some help, Dee."

Then she was gone.

My mother clicked her tongue audibly against her teeth, a terrible snatching sound. "Debbie bugs me," she said to no one.

"She was trying to help," Lia said delicately.

"Help?" My mother spat the word out.

"Dad says we have to pack. But you just sleep all day."

My mother fake laughed. "Is that what you think? That I'm up there resting? Hey. *Look* at me." My mother leaned forward. "Is that what you think?"

Another thing I would come to understand more deeply over the years and see in myself: the avoidance of a close friend, the inability to tolerate another person's happiness. That was the last time we saw Debbie. My mother was aware of her ability to drain and diminish, to pull others down with her. I was angry with Debbie for not seeing what I could: that my mother was only pushing her away because she knew she would have to say goodbye, and she wasn't strong enough for that. I wasn't naive enough to think she actually cared about Debbie insulting us, possibly hurting our feelings.

After that afternoon, my mother started locking the doors. She didn't let the neighbors come in unannounced, the way they used to. She didn't let them come in at all, ignored their looks as we packed up. When Debbie stopped coming around, my father mentioned that she must be envious of the new house. None of us dared correct him.

The house was in shambles. Every room was half packed, the boxes loaded with mismatched items. She threw away hundreds of things, random things, like night-lights and carrot peelers, things we would later search for, finding it easier to drop them in the giant black bags, out of sight, out of thought. We weren't prepared to leave, but had no choice with a new family moving in. My mother was stretched to her limits.

One afternoon, she chased Lia around the kitchen island, the vacuum held high in the air, its hose zigzagging like a snake, letting out its mechanical scream. There was nothing so frightening as my mother leaping across the tiles, so many parts of her trembling. She tripped and banged her mouth on the counter, ripped open her bottom lip. Stunned on the floor, she pressed two fingers to her mouth, lifted her hand to reveal the blood milking. "Look what you did to me," she said, pulling her lips apart to show us the split.

The next morning, the neighborhood mothers gathered around our small property. They hugged the four of us at once while the fathers offered pats on the back. We'd said goodbye to most of the kids the night before, and now they knelt in front of their windows, watching the moving van fill up with our things. Leo shrouded us in one of his grizzly bear hugs, and my father assured him we'd come back to visit.

I said goodbye to each of the rooms, all of them emptied out. They seemed smaller, bare except for the imprints of table legs pressed into the carpets. I pulled a pencil from my pocket and scribbled on the lip of the windowsill: *Anna was here.* I drew a ballerina, a pen, a book, until the wood was inscribed from edge to edge. I hoped a new girl might take my place in that house, feel at home and know its history, so she might carry it on. I liked this idea—a feeling that I was part of a larger sweep of time, stretching backward and forward over the days and decades, rendering me of little consequence, quieting the dramas of family.

PART II

Everett, Massachusetts

1974

The contents of the bag pool at her knees. Sitting, waiting, she twists the stems into bracelets. She doesn't know how to tie the knot, can't imitate the motions without her mother's fingers guiding her. *Ninna nanna, ninna nanna, baby's going ninna nanna*, she sings, thinking it will bring her mother back. Other times she is quiet, so that she might hear footsteps.

As the sky melts to black, the girl follows the route home until her eyes land on the front porch. Her father is standing behind the screen door in his holey T-shirt, callused hands on either side of his rounded stomach. He tells her not to hold her breath. He knew this day would come. But she sleeps on the front porch that night, curled beneath the mothy light. Calmed by the clinking and stamping of metal, the salty-sweet smell of peanut butter coming from the factory. She falls asleep thinking she'll wake to Mother's warmth lifting her off the porch, thinking she would never leave her out there like that, alone.

Daily, she runs to the field, the screen door clapping behind her like a fingers-crossed. She imagines a figure appearing at the edge of the grass, her mother's sundress coming into view, a long arm stretching, a hand reaching. She does this at eight, at nine, at ten years old, until her father demands her to stop. "She's not coming back."

ardboard boxes crowded the backseat, tilting and shifting with our possessions. We were on our way to the new house in Topsfield. My father had popped in Sofia's favorite children's cassette and we sang along as he thumped the steering wheel. My mother wore a large pair of sunglasses and cried most of the way. I watched her in the side-view mirror, removing the tears with frequent swipes.

We edged off the highway, the moving van close behind, and soon we were driving through a small agricultural town with countrified landscapes and tree-lined roads, brooks and streams crisscrossing the forest until they emptied into the Ipswich River. It was many miles of woods, and after that, many miles of corn-fields. Ford pickups in unpaved driveways, overworked men dressed in Carhartt pants. There were no commercial buildings—no restaurants or shops—only a post office, police station, and farmers' market. The neighborhoods spiraled outward from there, houses far apart, the elementary school embedded in the trees.

"Oh, that's great," my mother said, peering in the distance. "Just what I want in my backyard." The Danvers State Hospital loomed on top of a hill, its Victorian peaks stretching above the treetops. It had shut down in the early '90s and been converted to an apartment complex. A portion of the original structure still stood.

"It's nowhere near the house, Dee."

"My mother was in there," she said. "Not long after she had me. They locked her up in a cage. Nurses used to beat her."

We all gasped.

"A cage?" Lia asked.

My father swiveled his head in my mother's direction, gave her a look.

"They didn't know what they were doing," she continued. "The doctors made her crazy."

"They didn't lock her in a *cage*," he said.

"They did too. How would you know? You didn't know her."

"A cage, like, at the zoo?" Sofia asked.

"Is this really necessary? You're scaring them."

"She had epilepsy." My mother kept going. "My father pushed her off a cliff in Sicily. She landed on her head. Well, I don't know if that part's true."

"Did Nonna tell you that?" I asked.

She opened her mouth to speak.

"Hold that thought, Dee," my father said. "Here we go, everybody!" After another few seconds of trees, we pulled onto a barren development at the foot of a rolling hill range. Ours was the only finished house. It stood tall on a plain of gravel and dirt, massive and alluring. We ascended the long slope of driveway and I could almost smell the fresh paint. Beside me, Sofia bounced and kicked. "Everyone, grab one thing," my father said, and we climbed out, filling our arms with backpacks and stuffed animals from the backseat.

This was our first time seeing the house completed. Inside, sleek new appliances vied with traditional ceiling moldings. The walls were painted various shades of taupe with mud-colored trim; wooden floors the color of birch after rain. The way the first floor was designed—all arched openings and exposed beams— you could see into almost every room at once. My sisters and I ran to inspect our rooms, our duffels and backpacks thrown on the newly shined floors. When I came down some minutes later, I noticed my mother and father standing on the back porch, his sturdy hand on her shoulder as he ushered her around like a child. He pointed to the wide expanse of yard. "We can get a couple of birdfeeders here, Dee."

She bowed her head and wiped her eyes, but let him take her into a one-armed hug.

"Give it a chance," he said, offering her temple a kiss.

That night, I slept alone for the first time in my enormous new room, anxious, wishing I weren't alone. I was angry at myself for not being more independent like my sisters, who didn't seem to mind having their own space at all.

I thought about my grandmother in the mental hospital, lonely and confused, with no way out. When I tried asking my mother about it earlier in the day, she was cryptic, hesitant.

"Why did they put her in there?" I made sure to ask when Lia and Sofia weren't around, to fool her into thinking I was older than I was.

"She was really sad," she said, avoiding my gaze as she placed sweaters in her top drawer. "After she had me."

"But why would you be upset after a baby?"

"Chemicals, hormones. After the birth process. But it was more than that. I don't think she ever loved my father."

"How do you know?"

She shut the top drawer with force. "Are you done unpacking?"

"Were you sad after you had us?"

She gazed up at the ceiling, actually considering it. "No. Honest to God. I never had those feelings. Lots of women do, though." Her tone was soft and enlightening, briefly familiar, but slipped into something new when she took in the things surrounding her, the bins and boxes and piles of clothes. "Come on. I have to clean up." She shooed me out the door.

It was hot in my room. Even my eyelids were damp with sweat. Eventually, I dozed off, but woke feeling like I couldn't breathe. Bleary with sleep, I pulled myself out of bed and flung open the windows. Another hour or so of sleep, and then I woke to a chorus of clipping sounds, the humming of insects. I opened an eye and blinked, saw the moon's sprayed silver on the floor. The sounds only grew louder. I pulled the string on my bedside lamp and the room sprang to light. All around me, brown and black specks crawled. Moths and flies crept up the bed, across the walls and the ceilings. It looked like the room was moving.

I didn't want my parents to know I'd left the screenless windows open, the mistake I'd made. I ran to close them, swiped the insects off the blankets and onto the wood, their withered bodies coiling up. I waited for the moths to congregate at my bedside lamp, where I knew they would stay. Sickened by the bugs, I stripped my mattress and balled up the sheets, sleeping on the bare surface.

For a short while, it seemed the move had reanimated our mother, given her purpose. She spent a lot of time cleaning, decorating with cheap knickknacks. She even phoned a seamstress whose number she'd found in the local paper, asked her to sew drapes for each of our rooms.

While she organized and unpacked, we spent the summer exploring the nearby swamps. Cool mud splattered our legs and salamanders squirmed in our palms. We kept the creatures in shoeboxes filled with rocks and dirt—tiny homes we dampened with hose water. Lia placed the squirmy things on the inside of her arm. They crawled up and under her shirtsleeve, leaving trails of slime down her belly. No one paid attention to Sofia, who thought hers could swim. One night, my mother found her crying in the bathtub, a dead salamander floating in a cup of water, her pointer finger pressing its head beneath the surface. She thought she could drown it back to life.

We played on the front porch for hours, running from port to starboard, bellowing, "Iceberg, straight ahead!" We pretended we were stranded, rationed our food. We collected pine needles and acorns. Cracked the shells of redbud pods with our fingernails and pretended they were green beans.

When it rained, we played tricks on our mother, hiding in the crawl spaces of hallway closets, in the walk-in fireplaces, dusting our bottoms. Sometimes, to truly upset her, we ducked under the porch, sank our feet in the waterlogged sand until our legs shook and we could no longer feel our toes. Until she thought we had fled. She'd break into a panic, screaming our names at a pitch so piercing, the birds bolted from the trees. When we didn't answer, she called my father at work, frantic. "Vin, I can't find them anywhere. They're gone!" Hearing these words, a deep thrill would course through my veins, down to my toes in the mud. What if we really were gone? How far would they go to find us?

At the edge of the woods stood a wall of mossy stones, the remnants of old farmland boundaries. In the early evening, my father liked to stand on the back porch and look beyond the wall with one hand in his pocket, the other gripped tightly around the neck of a Budweiser, nostalgic for a time that was never his. He took us over the rock wall one Saturday, leading us through the abandoned trails to a gravesite from the 1600s. He held down sheets of paper on the headstones, mostly belonging to children, while we rubbed them with naked crayons. When we came back with our grave art, my mother made us throw them away, calling them morbid. My father didn't take us out there again. I kept hoping he would.

It was eerie in that house, too quiet, both inside and out. An occasional truck sped up our street just to turn around. There'd be a snip of music from the open window and that was all. We rarely left, especially when alone with our mother, trapped in a three-mile radius of construction sites and empty fields. We ventured out mostly to stock up on supplies in the neighboring towns. Nobody came to visit us. My mother had cut off ties with her friends, and it became an unspoken rule that we couldn't have anyone over.

There was a giant hole next door where a new house would be—two acres of crumbling, disturbed earth, surrounded by wetlands. We weren't allowed to go near it. "It's bad enough we're living here," my mother said. "Last thing we need is to be on the news because we let our kids fall in a damn hole."

For the time being, we were alone on our hill, except for the construction workers, who were already unearthing the lots across the street. If there was an emergency, my mother reminded us, daily, the police wouldn't know our address. We would have to give them directions and they might be too late to save us. Our lives were made up only of one another.

Once in a while, my mother traipsed outside to the sprawling dirt-lawn, came back with a bouquet of dusted coffee cups and burger wrappers, pausing to inspect each one as she dropped it in the trash barrel. "I guess the construction workers don't know how to throw away their friggin' Happy Meals," she'd say. "Think we're living in a dump." But she'd send me out there the next day to offer the men water bottles and turkey sandwiches, her way of flirting. Sometimes, I found her lingering on the front steps, sipping her iced coffee while she asked them questions about their progress, not listening to their answers, being girlish, smiley, toeing the velvety dirt.

The rooms seemed clean because they were empty. Upon closer inspection, you could see the tracks of our shoes in the kitchen, our grubby prints on doorknobs and walls. Little ant traps adorned every corner. The upkeep of the new house weighed heavily on my father, who worked desperately to maintain it. Empty rooms waited for furniture, and we were constantly told not to turn on the air-conditioning. To keep cool, my sisters and I took turns standing in front of the freezer.

He began to drink more and slept poorly. He suffered from night terrors, his horrific, deep screams booming down the hall. When we asked our mother the next morning why it'd taken her so long to wake him, to pull him from his nightmares, she didn't have an answer. He woke absurdly early each morning, grumbling past my room on his way to the kitchen. He was always working. And there were constant arguments about money. They tormented each other with shouting matches, or didn't speak at all. They tried slamming doors but the heat swelled the woodwork, catching them before they closed and taking the sting out of the violence.

One especially fraught afternoon, a month after we'd moved, my sisters and I were pinched together on the love seat because the big family couch hadn't come in. We were all tanned legs, knees knocking, skin peeling off the leather like stickers. We had the television sitting on a makeshift coffee table while we watched cartoons, fanning ourselves with the wings of torn boxes. I liked the darkness of the room—how it made you think you'd escaped the heat. We whined and moaned, lay on the floor with frozen packs of peas on our necks and stomachs. At the sound of rain pebbling against the windows, we cried out in praise.

Our cheering was cut by shouts from the kitchen. My father had come home from work to find a pile of unpaid bills stuffed in a kitchen drawer. My mother claimed to have put them there in an effort to keep the house neat. Even at age ten, I knew my mother didn't argue the right way. She lost track of the point, unable to commit to a single topic, made bad, nonsensical excuses, cried a lot. It didn't help that her nightgown was inside out and her lime-green headband was slipping off the back of her head.

My father was putting on a big performance with his "You're a moron" laugh, voice high with mockery. "I guess they were going to mail themselves," he said, smacking the envelopes against his palm. He got up, tried to get away from her to win the argument, but she followed, yelling insults at his back, calling him lousy and ignorant, a failure.

"I should be laughing at *you*," she yelled after him. "Where are my curtains? And my toilet seat covers?"

My father whipped around, teeth gritting, as if he were about to eat her. With one arm, he swiped everything off the counter. The empty fruit bowl teetered back and forth on the floor, laughing at him. He never laid a hand on my mother. But more than once he'd hurt himself, beating down doors until his hand busted through the panels, bloodied and bruised.

I listened from the living room. Lia was watching the television on high volume to drown out the noise while Sofia sat cross-legged on the floor in front of me, pleasant as a pretzel, her hand stuffed inside a bag of potato chips.

"Move over," I said to Lia. Beside me, her dirty foot inched closer. "You're grossing me out." I was trying to start a second outburst in here, to block out the other.

"Then go upstairs," she said. "I was here first."

"Why can't you just sit like a normal person?"

"Because. I'm comfortable like this." A worn-out *Pocahontas* Band-Aid dangled from her kneecap. I wanted to rip it off.

Lia didn't move, but swiveled her bright eyes in my direction. She was the only one of us with light eyes, blue-green like our father's.

"You're such an instigator," she said proudly, flopping back onto the cushions.

She was almost ten, about to start the fifth grade, but Lia was using words like "instigator" and wearing bras, even though she only had two cranberries on her chest. "Always stirring the pot," she had to add, trying to sound like our mother. She was impossible to argue with, too, unyielding. I couldn't get in too big a fight with her, otherwise it'd be awkward when I asked if I could sleep in her bed that night, which I'd been doing more and more. Sofia was quicker to say yes, but she kept me up with her scratching.

Sofia was the opposite of Lia. She still spoke in a pleading baby voice, asking Lia and me to play children's games with her. You could tell by the way she carried herself that she was enamored of her own cuteness, smiling after everything she did. She took one of the throw pillows off the window seat. Smiled. Sat on the floor. Smiled. Mousy, mushroom-shaped hair entwined in the back. "What's up, baby bro?" she asked when Beans sauntered into the room, his paws clicking on the hardwood. He plopped himself on the cool stone in front of the fireplace, his collar clinking as he panted. She slipped him a potato chip.

My mother kept shouting, and I decided to escape the madness on my own. I dug my nails into my skin. *Please don't let anything bad happen.* I whispered the words as I made my way upstairs, tracing my fingers along the walls. Most of the time, I wasn't sure what I was afraid of. But then came the fear of my father leaving us, a feeling of dread that seeped into almost everything I did.

Downstairs, the screen door ticked open and slammed shut. There was the dying noise of an argument. From my bedroom window, I could see my father making his way down the gravel path, arms swinging. It was almost seven o'clock. Where could he escape to out here? He hopped in the Chevy and I heard a few beats of "Wild World" as he reversed down the driveway, crunching rocks. I stayed there for a long time, watched a sheet of rain thicken as it traveled up the street. It streamed in rivulets down the uncurtained window until the outside world was a quivering haze, revealing only the impressions of things.

Maybe my father would continue down the winding roads, canopied by sopping trees, the seat belt alarm beeping until it merged with the music, becoming part of his soundtrack. Maybe there would be an accident, his truck lifted by a giant gust of wind and rain, flying through the sky into the hills with a loud crack. We could rush to the hospital together, where my father would be in bed, skin lacerated in purple and blue. He'd motion for us to come sit by his side. He would have hit his head, shaken his heart. He would be a new person.

12

Store owners wrench up their metal gates, rousing me from sleep. I'm comforted by the neighborhood sounds of waking, by the scents of sugar and dough drifting through my window.

I rise and everything rushes forward, bashing against my eyes. It takes me a moment to register the leather against my bare feet. I'm on the living room couch. My head pangs with the memory of alcohol, not enough water. I run my tongue over furred teeth, realizing I forgot to brush them. I've forgotten most of the previous nights. There was the walking to the corner store for cheap wine, then the TV going, then the walking back to the store for another bottle—a second, a third? I think it's Thursday. Lia called seven days ago.

I run to the bathroom and heave over the toilet, gagging tearfully. The color is a shocking, satiny red against the porcelain bowl. Emptied, I feel better. I wet my toothbrush and scrub at the maroon in the cracks of my lips until they're burning. In the mirror, I am jaundiced, smeared. My eyes haven't fully opened. I head to my room, to the warmth and the dark, when Vera barges through the front door.

Her eyes are black, her nose dripping. She blurts it out: "He cheated." She lets her tote slip from her shoulder, releasing a choking sob.

My eyes have regained focus. I feel renewed, provoked. I follow Vera to the couch, where she collapses into her own arms. It's as if I knew the whole time, by just the look of him, that he was bad news.

"I *met* the girl," she cries. "One of his friends from college. We spent like three hours on his couch talking the other weekend."

"Of course you did. When did it happen?" I palm her back.

"That's the thing! It happened *weeks* ago. When we first started dating. I can't even be mad at him."

"Says who? Of course you can be mad at him."

"He didn't have to tell me, though. He could have kept it to himself and I never would have known. That has to mean something, right?"

"You two were so serious from the beginning. He knew what he was doing."

"You don't even know. The part that really sucks?" Vera says, sniffling. "The part that kills me the most? Before we even slept together, I told him about my first time. I *told* him that it's hard for me to trust men. That sleeping together was a big deal."

She's referring to a night in our teenage years, the night of the bonfire, when a college kid kept refilling her cup. He lured her deeper into the woods, where no one could hear them. We were only thirteen or fourteen, never learned his name. I didn't think Vera could tell anyone but me.

She shifts and I realize I've stopped rubbing her back. "That's messed up," I tell her. "That's really messed up, Vera."

"But we're so close. We share everything with each other. A person can't fake that."

"You'd be surprised." The hand that was rubbing her back finds her shoulder. She's so rigid, shaking.

"Why would he do this to me? He asked me to move in with him. Why would he do that?"

"Because he wants to have it both ways. Most men do. Men are trash."

Vera jerks her shoulder. "Ow. You're hurting me." She leans back against the couch, pulls her knees up. "You think he doesn't really want to move in with me?"

"I don't know, Vera." I pretend to think about it. "Do you want to? Do you think you can trust him after all this?"

"I can't. I can't trust him," she says, crying harder. "Everything's ruined." She slumps into a ball and I open my arms for her to nestle into me. With Vera sad, needing me, I can be the friend I want to be.

"You don't need him," I say into her hair.

After Vera's breakup with Jonathan, I'm determined to make things right with her. We resume our picnics in the living room, breakfast sandwiches and coffees balancing on the leather stool.

We watch '70s movies starring Barbra Streisand, swoon over old New York. She interrupts one of the scenes to ask if I've reached out to my family. I tell her the call went straight to voicemail, and she accepts this.

I don't complain when Vera asks me to join her at the Christmas market in Union Square. We spend an hour browsing the stands, picking out things we don't need, reindeer ornaments and snowmen mugs. After, we find a cozy bar for popcorn and mulled wine. I am warm with alcohol, green lights, and Vera. We spend hours there, getting drunk and playing Battleship, cackling when Jonathan calls her three times in a row.

"Maybe he just wants to talk?" She's got the gentlest heart.

"Don't let him make you feel bad when he's the one that cheated."

Vera studies his name on her screen. I wish I knew what she was thinking about it.

I hold out my hand. "Give me your phone."

She does so without hesitating. I toss it in my bag, trying to hide my surprise.

For the next hour, the door jingles as patrons come and go. Outside, the snowy gray turns to black and it's a comfort to see our reflection in the window.

On the way back, we link arms, letting snow catch in our lashes. We collapse on the subway seats, laughing and pointing at our melty mascara. Vera kisses my cheek.

It's not yet six at night when I'm passing out from the wine and the hangover, my legs sore from walking. Lia and my father swirl around somewhere in my mind. I can feel myself slipping into that house, falling into a trance. I focus on the present. All the things Vera and I have fit into a day, the sound of her slurping lo mein on the couch beside me.

Next morning, Vera is by the kitchen sink. There's a quiet streaming from the faucet as she swirls a dish with suds. It's early and I am ten again, watching my mother clean. A feeling of release, as if I'm back where I came from, where I belong, cradled by Mother's crooning. *Ninna nanna, ninna nanna, baby's going ninna nanna.* I want Vera to take me in her arms.

She turns around when I pull out the stool. "Anna!"

"Dude, I'm so hungover." I lower my head onto the counter.

"Want cereal?" She grabs a bowl and starts pouring.

"How long have you been up?"

"A little bit."

I wait for her to say more.

She takes a spoonful of some healthy-looking flakes. I fill my own bowl and we chew in silence. "Do you like this stuff?"

"Jonathan called. Last night. He wants to take me to dinner."

I put down my spoon. "And?"

"I mean. It's a free dinner."

"Just tell me if you're getting back with him." I wipe an invisible splotch on the counter, studying the imitation granite. "You know what you're going to do. Just tell me." The back of my throat is tender. I can feel tears starting to rise. I'm embarrassed at my reaction. I want to have some say, some control. For her to care about my opinion. I should have stayed up last night, made sure we were on the same page.

Vera wipes her hands on her pants. "I know it's not a good idea."

"So, that's a yes."

"I'm going to try to stay strong."

"You're getting back with him."

She was pretending yesterday, wandering around the city with me. She was lying when she said she was happier without him. She was faking it.

"Whatever," I say. "It's your life. I won't be able to be nice to him, though. Not after what he did to you." There's a stubborn ache behind my eyes. I don't want this cereal. I let it get soggy in the bowl and I go for a walk. I know I'm making a fool of myself, that Vera will most likely report this to one of her work friends, but I can't control it.

I'm yearning for comfort, reassurance, someone to brood with me. How I long to watch my mother at the kitchen sink.

I head to my pastry shop, the one with the gleaming mugs and paper straws, waitresses playing cards at the back table. It's freezing outside. It feels like the air is destroying my lungs, shredding them to pieces. But I prefer this to the heat, just like my mother.

When I reach the pastry shop, it's empty except for an old woman in the corner. The overhead lights purple the knots of her fingers, shiny and bulbous. She brushes crumbs from her corduroy jacket. Her jaw slackens. Her wet mouth is full of croissant mush. She's all gums as she gulps for air in between bites. The sour scent of burnt coffee is making it difficult to breathe. She brings a mug to her burgundy lips, acrylic nails bending over her fingers, cracked and chipped—the polish a childish shade of pink.

Her silver eyes shine above the mug. I can't tell if her expression of contempt is real or if I'm imagining it. I can't tell if it's me she's staring at. She doesn't look away, and it doesn't seem crazy that she's watching me, waiting for me to a make a move.

Vera knocks on my door that night, comes in without waiting for a reply. She's wearing a long bathrobe and frog slippers. Her cheeks are scrubbed pink. The scent of cold cream relaxes me.

"Scoot," she says, and I slide closer to the wall. She settles next to me, wet hair spread out, cooling my forehead when it lands. "Tell me what's wrong."

When I don't respond she says my name, dragging it out like a song. She bumps her knee into mine.

I bump back.

"Anna, me getting back with him—it doesn't mean I don't want to hang out with you anymore. I love hanging out with you. You *know* that."

I nod, barely. If I try to speak, I'll start crying.

"I had so much fun yesterday. I want it to always be like that," she says. "And I want him to know you." She uses a couple of fingers to caress my arm. "I want the three of us to be able to hang out. Don't you?"

"Yeah," I say unconvincingly. "I do."

"We should do something nice. The three of us." She rests her forehead on mine. "You're my best friend, Anna. My sister. Don't be so sad." She wraps an arm around my shoulder. "I love you."

"I love you too," I muster timidly.

I want her to ask me about Lia, about my mother, to check in. I want her to take control. She offers me one last embrace and gets up, leaving the door half open.

I give Jonathan and Vera their privacy, trying not be bitter when I hear them laughing through the walls. Eventually, I fall asleep. When there's another knock the next morning, I can tell from the jokey rhythm that it isn't Vera's. I jump out of bed in a panic, hoping he won't just barge in. I fix myself in the mirror without turning on the light, try to be natural when I open the door.

He's in front of me, shining his wet, toothy smile. There's a spatula in his hand, and I can hear something going on the stove. "We're making pancakes," he says. "How many do you want?"

It appears I don't have a choice.

"We have bananas!" Vera calls out from the kitchen.

"I'll have a couple," I say, because it would be rude if I said otherwise.

Jonathan doesn't respond, but looks at me intently, in a way that unsettles me. It's enough to make me avert my gaze. I cross my arms over my chest, make a move to step into the hall, but he's blocking the doorway. He steps an inch or two to the right, still in the way. I wait for him to move, but he's just standing there. The light from the kitchen is bright behind him and he's a big silhouette. Finally, I hunch and brush past him, making contact with the skin of his hot arm.

Vera's sitting at the counter, neatly folding paper towels into triangles. She brushes my hair behind my ear when I sit. There's the smell of frying bacon, but it doesn't cheer me. Jonathan returns to the stove, reversing his cap and mouthing a song. I spend most of the morning avoiding eye contact with him, even as we eat across from each other at the counter. It occurs to me that I've never looked at him straight on.

"Wait, Anna," Vera says, dropping her fork with a clank. "What ever happened with your mom?"

All eyes are on me as I poke at my pancake, trying to think of what to say. "Oh, I don't know actually. I haven't heard anything."

"Did try you calling again?"

I run my fingers over my brows. My silence is enough to trigger her.

She has this look on her face, like she's mortified, like she's never heard of anything so terrible. "It's been over a week. What are you doing?"

"If she was dead, I would know," I mumble, not wanting Jonathan to think it's a big deal.

"That doesn't mean you don't have to call."

"I know."

"So why haven't you?"

"Why do you care?" My tone is harsh, but she's pushing me. She doesn't know when to stop.

"Why *don't* you care?" Without warning, she reaches across the counter for my phone.

"What are you doing? Vera, stop!" I lunge when she starts typing my password. Both of us are pulling on the phone, fighting over it, making a horrendous scene. Her fingers are tight and clammy. I take one and twist it, until she yelps and loosens her grip. I seize the phone and glare at her. "Now? Here? In front of *him*?" I can feel my face burning.

"We're not letting this go on," she says, turning to her plate, looking embarrassed.

I can hear him whispering to her as I storm out of the room. "She asked you to stop, babe."

I grab my coat and flee.

13

It looked like the sky was raining plastic and paper bags—garbage left over from the construction next door. Branches clicked against the windows. I fantasized about a hurricane striking Topsfield. My mother would fill a box with water bottles and peanut butter and bread. My father would pull out the road map and declare our escape destination. I could keep track of everyone in the car, the five of us with pillows and blankets stacked on our laps, Beans balanced on the center console.

We huddled at the table while my father worked on one of his projects, a birdhouse for my mother.

"Do me a favor, Anna?" He nudged his empty Budweiser with a pinky and eyed the fridge. I tossed the empty bottle in the trash, got another, watched as he took a swig.

"Want to try?" He held the bottle out to me.

"That's good, Vin," my mother said. "Real good."

I slunk low in my chair, telling him no, thinking it better to take my mother's side.

Beans was asleep under the table with his nose nestled between his paws, always wherever my father was. My father bought Beans on my mother's twenty-first birthday, the first year of their marriage. He came home with the dog's ears poking out from his flannel pocket, a big surprise. I wouldn't be born for another three years, but I still told people that story as if it were my own. "He was so tiny," I'd say to the girls in my class. "You could hold him in one palm."

Lia was hunched over a boiling pot on the stove, tasting the penne with a wooden spoon. A cloud rose from the pot and fogged up the windows. With the steam and the rain you couldn't distinguish the sky from the ground. Lia hummed, stirring the tomato sauce and kissing her fingers before capping it with a glass lid.

My mother pretended to supervise Lia, twisting around every few minutes. Sitting beside her, I could see that her green nightgown barely reached her knees. Her fleshy legs were swollen at the joints, pearl-blue knots running all the way down. "You're not dressing right," one of the old neighbors had said when she met my mother at the mailbox, right before we left Everett. "So big-chested—you should be wearing V-necks. Otherwise, you just look big." Now my mother was going through a phase of not eating, not cooking, then bingeing in the middle of the night.

Beans started awake, wheezing, letting out a wet cough.

"Anna, let him out before the rain gets worse?" my father asked.

I nudged Beans with my big toe and pushed him toward the back door. He pushed back. The cough erupted. "Seriously? This isn't normal," I said, disgusted. I directed the complaint to my mother because I was too afraid to address my father that way.

"Don't tell me," she said. "Tell *him*. It's not me keeping him alive. Dead dog walking."

My father didn't hear, pretended not to hear.

Once Beans was outside, the rain drowned his sounds. He remained planted on the steps, gaping and choking, silent through the glass. I stepped backward and out into the hall.

The only person Beans obeyed was my father. Sometimes, I caught him talking to the dog when he thought they were alone, tossing him scraps of prosciutto, even though it was expensive and my father reprimanded us for eating it too quickly. He'd lean down and grab Beans' ears, moving them around like two arcade game controllers.

I went back to the table. There was a clap of thunder and the windows rattled. Our gazes flicked to the bulb above us.

"Nonna and Nonno are bowling in heaven," Sofia said, because that's what my mother had told us when we were very little. My mother smiled closed-mouthed, went back to watching my father with her chin in her hands.

About an hour later, when my father finished the birdhouse, he got up without cleaning the mess. He settled in front of the television with a plate of pasta, leaving the rest of us to eat around his bits of wood and paint bottles. My mother was glancing around the kitchen, looking a little panicked. The chair scraped the tile when she stood.

"Where's the dog?" she asked. "Vin, is he in there with you?"

The fear came in a wave. A hot ringing in my ears. I glanced at the door, at my fingernails, back at the door. I crossed my fingers and shoved them beneath my thigh.

"Anna let him out like an hour ago," Sofia said.

I shot her a scowl.

My mother was too concerned to be angry. She yanked open the sliding door, called for Beans, distraught, forgetting that he couldn't hear. Rain drummed on the concrete outside. She returned two or three minutes later, hair dripping. "I can't find him." Her voice cracked. "He's gone."

"You checked by the woods?" my father asked, getting up from the couch.

"Yes! Will you help me?"

I prayed the chair would swallow me.

"Anna let him out before we ate," Sofia said.

My father made his way out of the living room and past the table, his eyes never leaving mine. "What's the matter with you? Huh?"

"I forgot," I said, over and over. All I could think to say.

"Of course you did," my mother said, stooped beside him, the two of them suddenly a team.

"It's not my fault!"

"Jesus," my father said. "Grow up, will you?" He was gone with a slam of the door. The little bird chime that hung on the knob rang out.

While my father searched, the rest of us remained in the kitchen. Sofia was lying in the dog bed, pouting, while Lia sat perched on the countertop, peeling string cheese. I had the sense that she wanted something bad to happen and for it to be my fault, though I had no reason to think this.

It was quiet except for the rain and the drone of newscasters coming from the television. My eyes worried the side door, where I waited for my father to emerge. When my mother started on the dishes, I snuck into the hall, stuffed my feet into someone's shoes, and slipped out the door.

Rain pelted my head and shoulders, striking like tiny rocks. I moved forward, startled by the long shafts of white-blue from the streetlamps. They cast shadows on the pavement like giant men in top hats. I was afraid to be out there, with water pooling at my bare ankles, my feet sinking in the muck. Across the way, in the neighboring lot, I could make out my father carrying a yellow ladder over his shoulder, rain assaulting his back. He was bent very low as he trudged through the mud.

The pit was over six feet deep, no doubt filling with water. My father slid the ladder inside and stepped down, appearing moments later with something in his arms. Watching him cold and desperate, I was smacked with the sudden feeling that I'd gotten the tragedy I'd asked for.

I made my way back to the house and waited inside, sopping wet by the door. "He's coming," I said, shivering. My mother and sisters rose from their grieving places. We heard the garage door opening, listened to his footsteps shuffling on the concrete. He paused at the stairs and we thought maybe he was taking off his dirty clothes. When my mother opened the door, my father was standing wide-legged with Beans in his arms, their foreheads pressed together.

"Is he okay?" Sofia said with her fingers in her mouth.

My father stepped inside. He lowered Beans to the floor and

under the light, and I saw that they were both covered in mud—my father's work boots, his pants, and his jacket. Beans was so dirty you couldn't see any of the spots on his neck and chest where the fur was supposed to be white. His wet hair almost looked like skin. With his limbs crumpled beneath him, I couldn't tell whether or not he was alive. A sick heat rose from my core to my forehead. Finally, Beans stood.

"You better get something to wrap him in," my father said to the room, making a rolling motion with his hands.

My mother gaped at the limping dog, who walked aimlessly, shaking.

"One of you get a sheet from the laundry room." No one moved, and his voice grew louder, threatening. "What'd I just say? Get a goddamn towel." Lia shot out of the room and up the stairs. I had never seen my father like this, vibrating with rage, his voice high then low, out of control. I slunk into the shadows.

"What happened?" my mother asked.

"He fell in the hole next door. Where the house is going."

She brought a hand to her cheek. "Jesus." She followed him into the kitchen. "You went down there?"

"I had to," he said. "It was filling with rain." He tore off a piece of paper towel and swiped it across his forehead. "I circled that area a dozen times. And then I heard him whining. Got a ladder." He tossed the paper towel in the trash barrel, avoided eye contact with us. "He was just sitting there. Stupid dog."

My mother crouched, bunching Beans in her arms despite the mud. "Why did you do that, Beansie? Why did you go down there? Want a bath, baby?"

Lia came back with a towel.

"Wrap him." My father's eyes were wet, maybe with rain.

I was sweating, tasting my own hot tears. My skin itched. There were a few minutes more of silent weeping. My mother and sisters made their way out of the room with Beans. A heavy, dripping arm cut in front of me when I tried to follow. "You stay here," my father said. I could feel the heat of his arm through my shirt.

Unlike my sisters, I was quiet, fragile. In the face of confrontation, mute. He pointed to the kitchen chair behind me and I dropped into it.

"I didn't mean to," I said, my breath coming hard and constant. I moved my fingers over the seat cushion, found a loose thread and pulled.

"Look at me," he said. "Look. Up. What happened? What did you do?" He stabbed at the counter with a finger.

Only a few months earlier we were sitting in his truck, his hand on the back of my neck. "He was taking too long," I said, wrapping the thread around my finger until it deadened. "I was talking to Mom. I came back inside and forgot he was out there."

"Don't do that."

I thought he was talking about the thread so I unwrapped it from my fingers.

"Don't blame your mother." He shook his head. "Just—" He waved a hand at me and headed for the sink. "I can't do everything on my own," he said, almost whispering. I braved a look at him. In that moment, what happened to Beans had widened, pooled. I didn't fully understand my father but knew I had caught a glimpse of something he hadn't meant to show me. He had spoken over himself, exposed something new.

He punched the faucet on, scrubbing at the mud and debris on his arms, bending low to wash his elbows. He muttered under his breath and shook his head. "Stupid dog. Goddamn stupid dog." He bent so low, I thought he might climb into the sink.

I walked a little closer, said his name like an unsure answer. "Dad?" He lifted his head to look at me, the first time I'd seen him cry.

The rain swept away and humidity enveloped the house, so thick I thought my arm could slice through it. My shirt stuck to my back; hair coiled around my neck like a rope. In my bedroom, I opened the window wider, inhaling the stony scent of rain. I stretched two hands out to cup running roof water in my palms. It would be easy for me to tumble through the gap and onto the sodden lawn. Would my father look through the kitchen window when my body dropped? Would he carry me to the car, whisk me to the hospital?

14

After escaping the apartment, I stumble down Columbus Ave until I'm drawn to the lights of a beauty shop. There's a cocoon of warmth when I cross the threshold, footsteps on granite tiles, a gleam from the shelves. I don't know the name of her perfume. Only that it comes in a slender chartreuse bottle, that it smells like lavender and apples. I used to sneak into her Everett room to use it.

I scan the rows and start grabbing at random. The first I spray on my wrist. It's too syrupy, not fresh. The next on my arm, too thick, too heady. The third I spray in the corner of my elbow. A deep vanilla. All wrong. I spray until there's not a patch of bare skin, until my sleeves are damp with mist, my nostrils tingling.

A male associate walks unhurriedly toward me, asks if I'm looking for something specific.

"I don't remember," I say, my voice breaking, eyes crossing from the alcoholic fumes.

I've been thinking about her too much; I don't have space left to worry for her. I know it's not the whole story, but my memory of her is dark and warped. It's bloated and twisted. A creature of its own. A malignance I've created that lives inside my head. I can't find her anywhere.

I miss my shift at the restaurant the next day. Did I even set my alarm? Three hours into brunch, I wake to three missed calls from my manager and a text from Tal: *Don't do this, Anna.* The more time that goes by, the more embarrassed I feel, the harder it is to respond. When my shift arrives, one day later, I don't show up.

We have to let you go, my manager texts. *Two no-shows? David's not having it.* And then: *I sincerely hope everything is okay.*

The first feeling that strikes is relief. I don't think about the money.

That night, sipping a mug of red wine, I pretend to read while Vera repaints the kitchen walls. She's been meaning to do it for weeks, sick of looking at the mysterious smudges and scrapes. I like the sticky pluck of the roller, streaks of eggshell white overtaking the room. The window is open and the heat is on high. The radiator's so close to my skin it hurts. I also like the way it feels—the slight burn blended with icy air. We haven't talked much since the incident with my phone two days ago.

"Are you working tomorrow?" she asks. Vera likes to visit when I'm at the restaurant, to eat lunch on my employee discount. I smile inwardly, knowing I'll never again smell the odor of garlic or feel the damp of sweat gathering under my arms. I hate that place—that pig of a chef, who's always squeezing my sides. *Eating a lot of fries lately. Huh, Ann?* And David—that crass bastard manager who shamelessly itches his balls in front of the female servers. My apron is crumpled on the chair across the room, ketchup stained, overflowing with pens and rotating beer lists.

I laugh without humor. "I was fired."

Vera spins around, her face stretched in horror—as if my firing, or getting into trouble, is a personal affront to her. "For *what?*"

I tongue the inside of my teeth, focus on the crooked tooth in the bottom row. "I missed a brunch shift," I say, in a tone that suggests she's overreacting. I pour another glass of wine that measures out to two. A few drops sink into the stone side table, the one Vera's mother gave us.

"What are you going to do for money? For rent?"

"I have a little in savings," I say, which is true, from working doubles. It won't last me forever—a few months at most.

Vera looks like she has something to say but stops herself. For the past two years, she's visited me at the restaurant dozens of times, securing a spot at the two-top by the side stations, letting me pick from her fries while I polish the silverware. She is probably wondering when this happened, how this happened.

"Anna."

I give her a grunt of acknowledgment. There are ripples in the plaster from where the walls have settled.

"What's going on with you?" She's off the ladder.

"You're dripping." I gesture to the eggshell splotches on the floor. She drops the roller in the tray.

"And what about home? You're not at all concerned?"

I make fingerprints on my wineglass.

I know what she's thinking. *She's your mother.*

Yes. But she's nothing like yours. You used to stare when she ate, I want to say. *You used to make a face if she got too close. You invited me to your house so you wouldn't have to come to mine.*

"You're being selfish, Anna. And cruel."

"Maybe I am."

She picks up the roller and turns back to the wall. "You're just like her, you know."

Blood rushes to my head. I feel my fingers clenching, my fists wanting to fight. "Fuck you, Vera." It's the first time I've said those words to her. I get up from the couch and rush past her. In my room, I pull my blankets over my body in a *whoosh*, ignoring the sting, the sheets that cling to the burn. How did I not feel my leg against the radiator?

Everything is fine. They would have called again. If something was really wrong, my father would have shown up at my door. The burn starts to pulse, probing layers of skin.

15

The new house was beginning to digest our lives. Throughout our first year there, the rooms, once large and vacant, had withered and cramped. A messy terrain of objects thrived beneath every bed and table. Drawers brimmed already with receipts, dried-up markers, and single socks.

My mother's behavior became stranger, her actions more erratic. She cried for no reason, or else she paced the halls like a ghost in search of something. Most nights, she stayed in the living room until dawn, entranced by the television. She opened the windows in warm weather, but remained indoors in the dark, listening to the sounds of summer. Wasting away with no reason to wash or dress, she fixed herself in the unlit corners of the house.

One night, lying in bed, I heard my mother talking to herself. I pinned my attention to the ceiling, trying to decipher her words. "Thinks he can keep me here," she said. "Thinks he can make me stay."

A chair screeched across the tile. The back door creaked and clapped shut, and I envisioned my mother walking down the moonlit path out back. What could she possibly be doing out there? I contemplated following her when two small bodies shuffled into my room. Sofia stopped at the edge of the bed, rubbing her eyes.

"What is she doing?" Lia asked.

Together, we tiptoed into the hall, following the swell of white coming from the big window. We watched quietly, Lia pressing her head against the glass. Sofia chewed her bottom lip, her delicate wet sounds filling our ears.

In the backyard, my mother paced in circles, her pale nightgown luminous in the dark. At the edge of the woods, tiny globes of yellow floated. They were lightning bugs—the first time I'd seen them, maybe my mother's first time too. She was mumbling unintelligible words, marble-mouthed, gripping her hair. I wouldn't have been surprised if she slipped into the forest on all fours to scour the soil and rocks.

I didn't think to disrupt the spell, to bring my mother inside. I felt safe with her being far away but still visible. I tensed when I heard my father step onto the back porch—his work boots biting into the wood. He cleared his throat, wet and whiskey-clogged, his drink of choice when he was out with coworkers. He didn't go to her. "What are you doing?" he finally said, not really asking.

In a rapid movement, my mother spun around to face the house, her eyes shooting up to the big window. The three of us dropped to the ground, limbs banging as we scrambled away.

That night, in my dreams, I heard the sounds of my mother whimpering and pacing, her bare footsteps muffled in the yard. The hem of her nightgown was grass-strained, dip-dyed green. Streaks of dirt climbed her pale legs. Drenched in a moon bath. A woodland fairy without wings.

It became her fascination—talking dreamlike of creatures behind walls, of porcelain dolls stirring at night, living in a world where the impossible could happen.

She was happier in colder weather. In the last days of fall, she sat on the porch swing, barefoot and wrapped in my father's corduroy jacket, looking out at the woods with the dog lying at her feet. "Where is everybody, Beansie?" she asked, offering him a lick from her yogurt cup. "You miss your sisters?" She rubbed his back with the bottom of her callused foot, a clear piece of tape stuck to her heel. Through the screen door we heard her call for us. When we joined her on the porch, she talked only to herself and the dog.

Smoke billowed from burning leaves in a distant yard. Even now, this is the most comforting scent I know. It reminds me of the hours we spent monkeying around on the railings, white tights catching on splinters, magenta-colored fingernails digging into soft pine—and as we got older, the three of us sitting cross-legged on the porch in our jeans and turtlenecks with *People* magazine resting in our laps.

"I'm going to put a fairy garden back here," my mother announced, rocking, unperturbed by the wind. "So the fairies will come."

Sofia looked to me, confused. Lia backed away, her heels crunching on dry leaves. As if she thought she would catch something.

A gust of wind and the gate swung open, clanked against the fence, several beats. We pinched our collars to keep warm.

"They come, you know. If you're real quiet. They wear flowers for clothes."

Sometimes, I'd recoil from her, unnerved by her fantasies and how easily she slipped into them, wishing for the mother I'd known in Everett. But there was something endearing about her, running her fingers from wrist to elbow in a nervous pattern. A part of me felt strangely powerful, more knowing, capable of disabusing my mother of her strange notions. Unlike my sisters, I was intrigued by her constructed universes. I wanted to know if she believed the things she said.

"Have you seen them? Do they talk to you?"

"Oh, yeah. I can understand them. I don't know if you'd be able to." She sort of shrugged, dismissive.

"Can Dad understand them?" I asked, knowing what I was doing, that I was too old to be asking these questions in any serious way. But she wasn't thinking about that.

She made a sound of disbelief, rolled her eyes. "You kidding me. He doesn't understand nothing, your father."

At the edge of our yard, orange slices beamed on the trees. She had pierced them on the branches days earlier, leaving them as an offering for the weaker birds that hadn't migrated before summer's end. She spread some of the pieces on the porch railing, hoping the birds would come up close. They never did. I inhaled the citrus smell, wafts of it feathering through the smoke. Pine cones lay scattered on the ground. She had glazed them with peanut butter and rolled them in a layer of seeds. Against the thick backdrop of woods, animals flapped and scurried. The forest was alive.

"That's what I'll do," my mother said. "Build a fairy garden." She nodded, as if we'd given her permission.

The four of us remained outside while my mother talked to the wind, until the pink sun receded behind the trees.

Eventually, we stayed away. Even Sofia stopped trying to climb on her, to lean against her while they watched movies. She didn't try to pull at her hair or trace her unruly brows with her fingers. At night, we didn't call for her when we woke from nightmares, but turned to each other, slipping into each other's beds. I tried not to linger on what was happening, consigning such things to some unreachable region of my mind.

Other times, she was outright cruel. One afternoon, when I was eleven or twelve, I lifted my arms to tie my hair when I noticed her watching me. Then she burst into choking laughter. "You're not shaving yet?"

I snapped my arms to my sides, each strand of hair suddenly noticeable against my skin. "I didn't know it was time," I said, hoping she might soften.

I suppose I did know, but she hadn't told me. And I liked the feeling—lying in bed at night, fingers curled in the warmth of my underarms, grazing the soft hairs.

"Use one of the disposable razors," my mother added. "In the bathroom closet."

As she leaned back in the chair, her legs met at the ankles, too thick to cross. I looked to her spot on the living room couch, at the dimple in the cushion where her body pressed into the leather day after day. A ragged green blanket spooled into a pile on the floor. It would be too easy to shame her back.

"You're like a man," Sofia said, laughing harder. Lia and Sofia giggled into their palms.

She lived for these moments—for the chance to pit us against each other. Still, we could sit with her for hours over Lipton tea and Italian cookies, repelled and transfixed by her need to be one of us.

At the time, I was reeking of self-consciousness. My skinny arms and shoulders constantly towed downward, shrinking. I was often told at school to "speak up," and got good at deflecting attention, at slinking away. I avoided my reflection in window fronts and hallway mirrors, beneath the overhead lights in restaurant bathrooms, which illuminated my worst features. There was something unnerving about my large eyes, my sharp chin, cheeks hollowed out. My hair was thin and flowing away; all you saw was face.

I'd become something foreign in my family, the odd one

sitting in the corner, eyes shiny like glass. We would watch horror movies together, my mother, my sisters, and I—the four of us pinned to the couch with our knees up, blankets spiraled around our legs for protection, even in the heat of summer. If a strange, spooky girl appeared on-screen, my mother and sisters would laugh and point and say, "That's Anna." I pretended not to mind, wearing this peculiarity as a badge. I refused to tease back. They were loud and opinionated. I was not.

I often wondered if there was a girl somewhere who shared this feeling of detachment from those she loved, from herself. Was there another girl who looked and talked like me, who performed the same actions as me, maybe at the exact same moment? Another girl drinking a glass of skim milk, sitting cross-legged on the pantry floor alone, eating handfuls of baking chocolate? Another girl looking out the passenger-side window of her father's truck, watching the raindrops race down the glass, feeling bad when they hit the bottom and lost their shape? If she did exist, I never met her.

16

Our third summer, we faced a landscape of oaks and emerald lawns, a scene of colonial homes with bald eagles above every door. We were surrounded by neighbors. They convened on patios with wine and cheese, their words turning into garbles as they moved into the night. The air in summer was thick with the scent of mulch and spent charcoal. Water hoses lay curled on sun-splashed driveways, bicycles tilted on the grass.

Though we were the first family to settle there, our own house seemed out of place. Perched at the end of the lane, it was not a home that drivers slowed down to admire. Paper shades, intended to be temporary, hung wrinkled and torn in every window. The front porch stood empty save for a single lawn chair, an old can of beer warm in the cup holder. There was no basketball hoop over the driveway, no flowers in the dirt lining the path to the house.

Next door, the giant hole loomed. In spring, the snow on the nearby hills thawed and flowed, flooding the property. The lot was later deemed uninhabitable, unsafe because of the wetlands—sucking mud, croaking frogs and bugs, and a strong odor emanating from the ground in summer. It was a rotting wound, torn open. Potential buyers soon realized this, so the land next to us remained untouched. The giant pit was an infinite thing, a reminder of a failure and a promise unkept.

One August morning, a U-Haul pulled up across the street, a red Toyota trailing behind. A girl around my age climbed out wearing headphones and bug-eyed sunglasses. I noticed the accessories first, then her figure—the long legs and torso, rounded thighs that touched. She was one year older than me, according to my father, who'd met the family some weeks prior, but she had stayed back a year. A thirteen-year-old who looked seventeen. She wore a lilac shirt that I would come to know well, made of a prickly material with sparkles sewn into the threading. When she raised her arms, the fabric lifted above her waistline, exposing a slice of creamy skin. I've thought of the scene many times since. I've altered it, placing the string friendship bracelet already upon her wrist, browned from never taking it off.

My cereal lay untouched in my lap, milk souring in the heat while I watched the girl gather her things from the passenger seat. Transfixed by the way she swayed when she walked, as if she knew someone was watching. She pulled a canvas tote over her shoulder, twisted blond strands into an effortless braid that cascaded down her back. She pressed a button on her MP3 player and, climbing her way up the lawn, extended her long, moley arms to dance.

Her mother called and the girl ignored her, skipping inside the double front doors. She burst back through them in minutes, huffed and collapsed on the front steps, resting her chin in her hands. She looked satisfied, pleased with her own mischief making as her mother chided her. I inched forward in my seat, trying to listen, shocked when the girl looked in my direction and waved. She was like that, able to move on quickly from upset and irritation. Nothing seemed to sink below the surface. I lifted my hand and returned to my cereal.

Vera's was a one-story home diagonally across the street, butter yellow with neat black shutters and a wraparound porch. By the front door stood a ceramic, curly-lashed cow, hand-painted by her mother. It wore boots and a cream bonnet, chewed on a sunflower stem. Chimes and colored glass dangled from the trees, flashing in sunlight. A blue-and-red Kerry-Edwards sign stood in the green lawn, which I mistook for their family name. She came along at exactly the right moment—climbing the yard as she danced to her music. She was sent there especially, for me.

In the days after she moved in, Vera and I spent afternoons subtly communicating, an unspoken game. I pretended to read on the porch while she listened to her music on her front stoop, the two of us waving hello and goodbye. One morning, I collected in a shoebox some of my favorite things—a packet of glittery press-on nails, Juicy Fruit, and a bag of worry dolls my father had brought back from Sedona. As Vera watched me from her stoop, clad in her denim skirt and purple sandals, knees swaying, I made my way down the steep lawn and placed the treasures in her mailbox. Once I was back on my turf, she zoomed across the grass, lifted the lid, and searched inside, hungrily, never tentative about the pursuit of pleasure.

The next morning, she left something in my own mailbox: a navy clutch filled with seashells, a mood ring, and an opened pack of candy cigarettes.

It's likely that Vera detected my lack of confidence, hiding behind my book and my hair, my tiny offerings in the shoebox. I couldn't believe she wanted to be friends with me. I was ugly with thick brows that touched in the middle, a giant space between my front teeth. Maybe she sensed that I was impressionable, easily influenced, so she latched on, relishing the prospect of her control. Not long after the gift exchange, Vera came right over and sat next to me on the porch. We became inseparable.

Daily, she charged up the front steps, cheeks marbled pink and white. Her fingers were marked with tan rings, a girl who could spend hours baking sleepily in the sun. There was the time she laugh-cried as her mouth became tethered to the bedroom carpet, her braces chained in thread. All the hours we spent on her trampoline—our hands dusted in a layer of citrus from grapefruit we devoured earlier.

Our bond was accidental, one that wouldn't have existed had she not moved in across the street when we were girls; a relationship that wouldn't have stuck were it not for the adhesive of that history.

At that age, she liked to point out what was wrong with me. She told me my brows were too close together, so I let her pull me into her mother's bathroom, sit me on the toilet, and pluck for an hour, while we sang along to the Black Eyed Peas. She told me I was flat and should be wearing two bras to give myself more shape, so I did, letting the straps carve a place in my skin. "I'm not trying to hurt your feelings," she'd say. "It's just for now. Until they grow." I believed she wasn't trying to offend, was only trying to help, the way girls do at that age. She told me my feet were big, but that was okay. It meant I would be tall.

In her house there were books. Stacks of them on window-sills, side tables, at the bottom of the stairs, books about politics and history and novels by writers Vera wasn't allowed to read yet because her mother said they were "for adults only"—books by John Updike and Anna Salter, Erica Jong and Alice Walker, most of them writers I wouldn't read until college. On rainy days, we'd sit in the velvet armchairs on either side of the built-in bookcase, beneath the yellow light of a floor lamp, the latest *Harry Potter* gripped in our palms.

Vera's mother, Natasha, kept healthy snacks in their cabinets, offered us peanut butter on celery stacks, handfuls of almonds and dark chocolate. Natasha was strong and clean—the high points of her cheeks radiating from daily lemon waters and vita-min C serums. She was in her early forties when she gave birth to Vera, spent years marrying and divorcing twice, refining her skills in ceramics, eventually opening her own boutique on the Salem waterfront—all things my mother disparaged her for. She moved to Topsfield so they could be closer to Vera's maternal grandmother, close to family.

As young girls, we could talk to Natasha. We could share our anxieties about sex, our bodies warping, handling unthinkable things, and she listened to us with thoughtfulness, charmed by our naivete at thirteen, fifteen, seventeen. It seemed my mother was forever waiting for me to grow on my own. And she wanted nothing to do with Natasha. We were invited many times for sunset dinners on their back deck, but it never happened. My mother was afraid of being judged, probably because she judged so much herself. She suspected other women were out to get her.

Vera said things like "Your mother sleeps a lot." She asked what she did for a job though she knew the answer. "She's funny," Vera added. "She tells really good stories. I love the sound of her voice, that accent." Vera's mother didn't have an accent. She was born away from the city.

Alongside Vera's house, next to the garage, sat a sunken trampoline obscured by a bed of hollyhocks and lavender bushes. This is where we spent our time, Vera and I, hours on that trampoline, the hems of our tank tops looped into our shirts like bikinis. There, we jumped and lay down and daydreamed together. Vera took advantage of my passivity, my inability to object to anything, even if it meant suffering in her yard in the summer heat with allergies that made my eyes swell shut. Always, I was the one to take the necklace with the missing bead or the more melted popsicle. I waited to offer, knowing that I could not bear the silence, the prospect of displeasing her. I let her tease me for my inelegance and gullibility. I let her call me a baby. I let her boss me around. One day, I would grow bitter, my anger a slow burn, something I stowed away and would hold on to for years. But back then, nothing would tear me away from her. Vera, my first friend.

17

I'm on the fire escape with a mug of red wine, my third, wrapped in a throw that's never been washed. The sky is a creamy aerated pink, calling attention to itself. It's too warm for winter. Noisy birds scuttle. It feels like the end of the world.

There's a knock at the door. Squat in the peephole, Jonathan shifts from foot to foot, a black gym bag slung over his shoulder. He has a flower bunch nestled in the crook of his arm. I let him inside and he follows, traipsing through the cluttered apartment. It only looks this way because Vera is at work. While he explains that he thought she'd be home, that he'd wanted to surprise her with his purple tulips, I finger-comb my hair into a messy bun, use my shirtsleeve to scrub my wine-stained teeth.

"You can wait for her," I say. "She might be stuck on the train." I swipe another bottle from the counter, climb back through the window.

Doesn't he know a thing? Vera hates tulips.

He drops his bag on the armchair and invites himself on the fire escape. Before long, he's gulping back my wine, cracking jokes about how he found me drinking alone. I feign smiles for the better part of an hour. I think about the time he wouldn't move from the doorway, his bullying glare. His demeanor now seems mostly harmless, and I think maybe he's on his best behavior after his lapse.

From my spot on the fire escape, I can see the purple petals splayed on the counter, the flowers still in their plastic wrapping. How often men perform from the same script. I pity Vera and her tendency to ignore the gross parts of people, of Jonathan—his unprompted advice about finding jobs in New York, his self-centered asides, the unwanted flowers. He probably can't tell I'm not listening.

He's okay-looking with his beard, with his hair a little grown out. He's an inch shorter than me, but sitting he is several inches taller. This seems to give him confidence. He's less aware of how he carries himself when he's drinking, finding reasons to touch me, tapping my arm with his knuckles when a nod would be sufficient. The more he drinks, the more he looks at my mouth. Caught in a place between repulsion and intrigue, I pull my lips into a pout, start enunciating with care. At times, I lose my nerve. I have to look at my hands when talking to him, scrape out the lines of brown that live beneath my nails. He pops into the apartment, grabs another bottle. When he comes back, there's a shift.

"You're not the way Vera says you are," he says. I think it's meant to be a compliment.

"What does Vera say I am?" Layers shed as I drink, like a molting snake. I'm wearing an oversized nightshirt, loose on the neckline. The fabric slips down my arm when he bounces his shoulder into mine.

"You're always cooped up in this apartment," he adds. "You never come out of your room. You should hang out with us more," he says, taking another sip. "You're fun." He raises a brow, parts his mouth crookedly. "You just have to, I don't know, let loose."

It's their nerve that grates—this thinking they know me better than I know myself. I study a drop of bird shit on the railing because I'm not sure what to say. The sun is sinking behind the rooftops in a blaze of dying light, momentarily blinding.

"You're empty," he says.

I'm not sure what he means. He lifts the wine bottle, pouring the last of the grainy liquid into my cup. Is this the second or third time he's done that? I'm swaying, smiling for no reason.

"Whoops," he says. "All out."

Back inside, wavering in the kitchen, Jonathan refills his mug with a new bottle, starts to top mine off. "No, no. I am *done*." I laugh, shielding the top of my glass.

"Is that right?" He puts his hands on my shoulders, trying to steady me. His hands are too big for his wrists, white and smooth, as if he's never done a day of real work in his life. "One more for me," he says, taking a long sip, watching me with one eye. "You're beautiful," he says, leaning clumsily against the counter. "But you know that."

"Okay, Jonathan," I say, thinking he's such an idiot. Thinking, if I kissed him right now, he wouldn't hesitate. He wouldn't care about Vera. Not for a moment.

Outside, the street's lively. There's the buckle of cars, the din of voices.

I don't even do anything. I don't step forward or back. And I know that because I do not move, because I do not make a decision, he is going to kiss me. I wait for him to come. My gaze drops to his lips. He steps closer, strokes my throat with his thumb. His mouth collides against mine and I let him guide me to the sofa, let those too-white hands pinch my nipples through my shirt. It's dark and my ears are buzzing. Before I know it, he's pressing his warm, wet dick into my palm. I shove him, make a small sound of protest.

There's the sound of a bag hitting the ground. Then the look on Vera's face, her wrinkled chin, features plummeting in a single, horrified motion. She flees the room and Jonathan leaps after her, clumsily pulling up his pants. I reach for sobriety, but it's no use.

18

I wanted to find my mother. I rooted through her things, desperate to discover more of her, to know her before we became her life. My parents' room was a repository of things, mountains of clothes and bags, still-packed suitcases, piles mysterious and untouched. I tore through satchels and trunks, clothbound boxes with golden latches, velour pouches at the bottoms of drawers. I turned through greeting cards stowed away in her bedroom closet. I wanted to know if she made people laugh, what they would always remember about her, if she had any secrets. I wanted to know what she was like in a group of girls—whether she was the one to walk a few steps ahead, like Lia or Vera, so that she was in plain view, or if she'd been more retreating, like me. Mostly, I wondered if my mother and I would have been friends.

I searched for some kind of beauty, poring over old albums and class photos. The girl I tried to re-create never had a face. Flipping to my mother's photo in the yearbook, I discovered it scribbled over in green ink.

Lia and Vera taught me everything—how to apply winged eye-liner and dab fragrance behind my ears, how to dye my hair from the box. If we ordered pizza, it was one of them who called to place the order. Lia looked older than me too. At twelve, she started getting a butt, wearing thongs she bought at the mall with her allowance. She kept them hidden in a trunk under her bed and didn't think anyone knew about them. That is, until my father walked past her bedroom one day, spotting a lacy thing on her carpet that none of us had noticed. It seemed my father had almost forgotten how to breathe, spit catching in his throat. He turned around quickly, disregarding whatever it was he'd come to tell us.

We didn't find out that Lia had her period until six months after the fact, when my mother discovered a box of tampons in Lia's closet.

And when my time came some months after that, I turned to Lia for help. She stood outside the bathroom, issuing instructions while I tried to insert the applicator. "Put one foot on the bowl," she said through the door. "Try different angles."

I could hear Sofia cracking up as I stood on one foot, trying to implant the small pipe of cotton. Once inside, it felt larger than it was. The plastic casing didn't slide in easily, like I thought it would, and kept prodding at my insides.

"It won't go!" I said, laughing to disguise the panic.

"Just push it up there, Anna!" She opened the door and I

scrambled to pull up my pants, a half-bloodied tampon pinched between two fingers.

I was thankful for the sympathy in her voice. "Here. It's easier if you lie down the first time. That's what Rachel's mom said."

It upset me that she'd gone to another mother for help. That meant Rachel had known too, before me.

"Come try on the bed. Don't go anywhere, Soph. You'll need to learn this too."

I worried about Sofia. At ten, she seemed like she would never grow up. Her raging skin inhibited her. The doctors were sure she would grow out of the eczema, but the fabric of her clothes clung to the open wounds, and if she tugged a shirt off too quickly, layers of skin came with it. You always knew when Sofia was in a room, a muted scratching sound marking her presence.

She was terrified of our father, tense when he entered a room. He'd take hold of Sofia's arm and yank up the shirtsleeve to inspect the skin, stippled in bleeding scabs, then reprimand her for not taking her medicine. She hated the way the prescription cream made her feel, so she never put it on. Against Sofia's will, my father coated her in beeswax—a special treatment he found after hours of scouring the web on the family computer, an old Dell he brought home from the office. After a fresh coat of the beeswax, he'd bind her arms and legs in plastic wrapping. She held on to him while he swaddled her legs, her fingertips pressing into his shoulders, eyes glossing over from the sting. She sucked in a breath of air, and though I felt for her, I somehow managed to feel envy at the attention she was getting.

It seemed to me that Sofia was averse to her own body, believing she would always look that way, and I suppose my father's attempts at caring for her turned physical affection into something like an invasion. I understood and tried to be kind to Sofia, complimenting her larger-than-normal eyes and her curly hair. I could tell from the way she covered herself in the dead of summer that she didn't think she'd ever be pretty, didn't expect to be admired by others. She even transformed her room into a shrine to her former self: baby pictures taped to the mirror, stuffed animals on the bed, baby shoes hanging from hooks on her wall—Sofia's name embroidered on their heels in bright pink stitching. On her nightstand sat a tiny ceramic box that held every one of her baby teeth. Pearly bitty bones, turned gray at the roots.

It was our third year in Topsfield. Throughout town, lampposts were wrapped in warm-colored leaves, porches decked with mums and witches. The few restaurants in town boasted of their autumn-themed stews. In September, it still felt like summer, but everyone was in a hurry for change. Unable to picture the Everett house as clearly as I once did, I longed to smell it again, the damp rot.

Sofia's room had become my favorite spot in the house. When she wasn't home, I'd read library books on the window seat, turning the pages slowly, relishing the crinkle and smell of protective wrap. My own room was overcrowded and stagnant because I neglected to clean it. I stowed snack wrappers and soda cans in my drawers, stuffed wads of worn underwear in the back of my closet. I never wanted to be in there.

We were all in Sofia's room one afternoon—Lia slumped on the beanbag chair, Sofia next to me on the bench. Across the street, we could see Natasha swaying on the woven hammock in a bright yellow sundress. She was peeling an apple, her movements rhythmic and hypnotic. Thumb pressed against the blade, sinking into apple flesh. A loose French braid draped over her shoulder. I watched, imagining what it would be like to have her as my mother. Graceful. A woman you wanted to be like.

She reached her arm toward Vera, who sat nearby on the steps, picked up a strand of her hair, and twirled it around her fingers. I could almost hear the words *my baby girl.*

Lia, Sofia, and I despised that gesture. Mothers who moved toward their daughters with their arms outstretched, calling them baby. We pitied girls who had these mothers, who were constantly told how lovely and loved and special they were. We laughed at them. "What babies," we said. "They'll never grow up." We wanted to believe our way was normal. We didn't need to be coddled. We could fend for ourselves.

A sound came from the hall. The snap of my mother's ankles and knees. She loomed in the doorway, lines from the bedsheets imprinted on her cheeks.

"You guys," she said. "Look what I just found. You're going to *die*."

She held a photograph to her chest—she and our father at the docks in downtown Hyannis. In the photo, my mother was striking a model pose with her butt jutting out, one hand on her hip. My father lifted his sunglasses, eyeing her, entranced.

There were other pictures strewn about the house—on the fireplace mantel, the side table in the foyer—but never a photo that captured my parents this unguarded. In this particular shot, my mother wore white high-waisted pants with pale yellow stripes. Blush warmed the tops of her cheeks. Her hair was the color of dried apricots.

"See?" she said, hovering over me. "See what I used to look like?"

"I can see it, Diana," I said. Calling our mother by her first name was something we habitually did now, a pattern that strengthened as we got older, taller, bigger than our mother. It was a challenge she refused to acknowledge.

"You didn't even look," she said.

"How long do you want me to look for?" It was uncomfortable, sad, seeing how much she'd changed from the person in the photo. I didn't want her to see that sadness in my face.

"I wish I'd kept those pants," my mother said. She glanced at herself in Sofia's full-length mirror.

Lia sank low in the beanbag. She'd slashed her jeans full of holes with a razor, and was now drawing on her exposed knee-caps with a pen, not paying attention. I straightened on the window seat, feeling alert to the tension in the room. "Hey, Diana," I said, trying to divert our attention from her body. "Can we get a hammock?" I pointed out the window, where Natasha swayed, her dress bunched at her thighs.

My mother cleared her throat and looked at the photograph

once more. "All right, well. That's all I wanted to show you." She made her way out of the room.

Over the summer, we'd installed an in-ground pool—a big deal for our father, who maybe wanted it more than we did, to prove to himself that he could have one, though we could scarcely afford it. My mother no longer owned a bathing suit. The last few times she sunbathed on the deck, she hid beneath her black cotton shirt, sweating. When she couldn't stand the heat, she stepped into the pool with her clothes on.

Whenever she stood in my doorway asking how she looked in a dress, whether she should straighten her hair, I had no answer, couldn't understand why she fretted about these things, when her troubles and repressions, to me, seemed much deeper. Something that no dress or swipe of makeup could conceal. I resolved that she wanted it this way, wanted her body to trap her in the house, in herself, to keep her from the outside world.

And I began to hate the changes happening to my own body—the skin that swelled beneath my bra straps, the pouch of my stomach, the tremor of my thighs—tried to control them by resisting them.

Influenced by my mother, I grew suspicious of every girl or woman I met, convinced they could not wait to identify my flaws, to put me down to elevate themselves—as I had been trained to do. She especially loved to talk about Vera. I think she knew that Vera was more put together than we were, was prettier, which somehow reflected negatively on her as a mother. So she disparaged Vera in my presence, maybe trying to lift my own confidence. But her efforts created a reverse effect. They made me weak and self-conscious, fearful of other women and their punishing instincts, made me envious of Vera and her charm and self-assurance.

I buried my voice to be the opposite of my mother; I withdrew more. At school, at least once a week, the hockey players swooped behind my desk, hissing at the back of my neck. "Do you talk?" Their hot breath lingered on my skin, laced with the scent of onion chips. They poked me, clapped in front of my face. "Are you a mute?" Girls would press their foreheads together, often whispering in tones that were meant to be overheard. "Her whole family is weird," I heard them once say. "Have you seen the mother?"

The way she ate disturbed me. It was like she was showing too much of herself, like she was something primal, indiscreet. I balked at the way her tongue poked out of her mouth as she ate too-big leaves of lettuce, or the way she relentlessly asked if you wanted to try her meal so she could take a stab at yours. She made me instantly aware of my physicality, the outline of my every movement. I came to learn that the more you were repelled by something, the more space it took up in your head.

She became larger, swollen, eating as if she were trying to shove something down. One night, that fall, I found her standing in front of the kitchen sink, her pallid face reflected in the window. She was studying something, turning it over in her hands with precision and care, as if it were precious. She was alone, and hadn't yet noticed me come in.

Gradually, she bent forward, dug into the thing with her

teeth, a purple plum. She devoured it, tearing at the skin, sucking the meat of it. She chomped so wildly that she swallowed the
sticker. She tossed the pit in the trash and slammed the can shut.
Next, she dove into a bag of mini croissants, shoveling them into
her mouth soundlessly. She spun around, filled with shame. Her
mouth and cheeks gleamed with perspiration.

I asked my mother to tell us about the day she and my father
met. Her face lightened as she began the heroic tale, as if she'd
been waiting a long time to tell it. She'd been sitting on the
porch at five or six years old, when a little boy from the neighborhood strolled into her yard. "Well, we called it a yard," she
said. "But we just had cement and dirt and some weeds growing
in the cracks. Me and my cousin Rose used to be so creeped out
by this kid because he smelled like pee and had holes in his
clothes, and he used to walk around with this huge stick. Don't
ask me why—no one knew what the friggin' stick was for. Everyone used to make fun of him. Anyway, all of a sudden he comes
up to me, and he's trying to take whatever I'm playing with out
of my hand—I don't know, probably a yo-yo or something. And
I tell him to go away and he gets right in my face and I scream
at him to get out of here and he just charges forward and bites
me right in the eye. Or, like, my cheek."

At this part, my sisters and I lost ourselves in laughter—eyes
streaming fat tears, stomachs aching so tight we had to grab
them. We laughed so hard that no noise came out, not because

it was funny, but because it had happened to her. That's how things worked in our house. Our mother told us stories of her being mistreated for our own amusement.

"It's not funny," she'd say. "I have a huge mark right here in my first-grade picture." She'd point to show us and we'd laugh some more. Then the story took a turn. The next afternoon, it was my father throwing down his bike, marching over to the boy. My mother recognized my father, who lived a few streets over, in a nicer house. Word got around about the eye-biter and my father decided to put a stop to it. I pictured him puffing out his chest, rising on his heels. "You better stay away from Diana Ceccacci's house, or you're going to get it." The boy never came back.

My mother waited years for my father to ask her out. They'd gone to the same school and been in classes together. Despite his valor that day in the yard, he was awkward, shy, but my mother liked that. At fifteen, he found the courage to ask her to the movies. *An American Werewolf in London.*

Not long after my mother showed us the photograph of her and my father, I spotted something different, off-kilter about the house. Making my way through the rooms, I searched for a new decoration or piece of furniture. I realized there were empty picture frames on every shelf, desk, and side table—clear glass windows where photos of my mother and father had once been. They were gaping white, begging to be seen.

I found her in my secret spot—her gray silhouette stamped

on the white curtains of Sofia's window seat. I joined her on the bench, setting down my book in the space between us.

"How did Sofia manage to get the best room in the house?" my mother asked, as if it were the first time the thought had crossed her mind, when, in fact, we had argued about it for days.

"Because she's the favorite," I said, pulling my knees closer to me.

"Oh, cut it out," my mother said. "I'm always equal with you three."

She was running her fingers over the curtains, inspecting the fabric. These same curtains used to hang in the front parlor of the old house. My sisters and I would slip behind the drapes so that only our socks were in view. We called out to her, giggling, readying to unveil ourselves. When her footsteps rounded the corner, we began our march, a spray of tissues in each of our hands. *Here comes the bride, all dressed in white.*

"Remember when we used to pretend we were getting married?" I asked her.

"You ruined these curtains," my mother said. "Some of the stains never came out."

"Yeah, but you used to laugh," I said.

"I did," she said. "I did."

I absently tapped on my book.

"That house," my mother said fondly. "That tiny little shack." She sat transfixed for a moment, picking at the strands of her hair. "I didn't want to leave, though. It was ours." Her eyes glazed over, drifting to someplace else. "This house still doesn't feel like ours. Three years later."

I nodded in agreement. "Too big."

"There's creepy sounds at night."

"Echoes," I said.

"Your father says it's the house settling into place. I don't believe him." She let out a quiet laugh. "Listen to me. So ungrateful."

"You didn't ask to move," I said, feeling good about the conversation, hoping to have some kind of breakthrough. It surprised me when my mother chose to defend him.

"Your father was trying to do the right thing. I bet if we were still there, I'd be complaining anyway." She laughed again, pulled her hair to one shoulder, inspecting the split ends. "I'll never be happy. It's how I'm wired. Watch out you don't have it."

I smiled in a sad way.

"Your father asked me to marry him in that house."

"I didn't know that."

"He was doing the renovations on a weekend, plastering the walls and all that. I was sunning on the front steps waiting for him to be done—no one lived there yet—when all a sudden he was calling for me. I told him I didn't want to go inside. It was a friggin' sauna. A mess. None of the lights were working. But he kept hollering so I went in and saw him standing there on the ladder, waving me over. I got all suspicious, was asking him what he was doing. 'Just get over here.' He was laughing. He started coming down the ladder, covered in white paint, sweating. A total nervous wreck. Then I saw this dandelion twirling in his fingers—my favorite. And there were dandelions in dirty glass bottles on the mantelpiece. Dandelions on the floor. He handed it to me. Then he pulled the ring out of his pocket. Can you believe it?" She let out a laugh that sounded cracked, throaty. "Nut job, he is. But I guess it was sweet."

"It's cute," I said, really thinking it.

"Then he told me he bought the house. That the renovations were for us. I thought it was just for his work. I was so happy. My first house."

I picked at the seat cushion. "Mom. The pictures, downstairs. What did you do with them?"

"I put them away."

"Why?"

My mother sighed. "I don't know. He pisses me off, Anna."

I gave her a look, suggesting that wasn't a good excuse.

"Bet you he won't even notice."

19

It was a brutal December. The mornings were bleak, soulless and frigid, and my mother didn't challenge Sofia and me when we shuffled into her room at half past six, still in our pajamas, pleading to skip school. "Fine, but don't get me in trouble," she said. "No telling your father."

Lia didn't want to stay home with us anymore. She seemed disdainful of the invitation, rolling her eyes and mumbling a judging "No, thank you." She was more social than us, had a group of friends who'd be waiting for her in between classes.

We sat in the front room, crafting paper snowflakes. The heat was on low and the house didn't feel much different from outdoors, but the Sinatra Christmas album playing in the background was comforting. Bowls of homemade stracciatella soup, a reward for staying home with our mother, kept us warm.

We were sitting on the rug, Sofia being dramatic about the temperature, cocooned in a queen-sized bedspread, rocking on her knees. "It feels like Alaska." She was wearing one of our father's sweatshirts with the drawstring tightened all the way, the hood taut around her head. She resembled some kind of earless sea mammal.

"Come on, Soph," I said. "This was your idea." I tossed the scissors in her direction, along with a half-snipped snowflake.

She groaned theatrically, pulled the blanket over her head. "Diana!" she cried. "Turn on the heat."

My mother was sitting across from us in her pea-green coat. "No way," she said. "Dad says we have to conserve. If we turn the heat up too high, he'll have a conniption."

Sofia lifted the blanket so that only her eyes were visible. "I don't see Vin around here. Do you, Anna?"

"It's not happening," my mother said. "Then I'll be the one he yells at when the bill comes. You're not supposed to be home anyway," she said, hoisting herself off the floor and onto the velvet love seat. "I don't like the snowflakes. I told you. I like classy. Simple stuff." She sat with her thighs splayed, her little feet crossed at the ankles. "Garlands and white lights." I pretended not to notice when she reached into her robe pocket for a pill. She kept it in her hands for a few minutes, waiting for me to look away. So I did, to spare us both the discomfort.

"I always wanted to do a can tree, though," she continued. "My grandfather worked at Sexton Can, and when my mother was little, he brought home cans in different colors and sizes and that's how they decorated the tree. With tinsel. You're not even listening to me."

Sofia was sifting through the box of decorations we'd pulled down from the attic. Suddenly she gasped. "I remember these!" In her hands was a glass Italian farm girl, dressed in green. "She was my favorite." Sofia hugged her. "Why aren't they out?"

My mother shrugged. "I couldn't find a place for them."

"They're going to get ruined in here."

Sofia started pulling them out, one by one. She and my mother chattered on, and I glanced out the window, where clean snow piled against the glass in luminous white mounds. I spotted our neighbors, Mike and Carol, sitting on plastic lawn chairs in the middle of their garage. They wore mittens and Patriots beanies, a fleece blanket draped across their laps. They sipped on Budweisers as they watched the snowfall. I'd heard my parents say their oldest son was serving in Iraq, or maybe it was Afghanistan.

"Aw. That's kind of cute," I said.

"He cheats on her," my mother said without looking out the window.

"How do you know?" I asked.

"He comes home all odd hours."

"Doesn't he work at Mass General?" Sofia said.

"And she's not much to look at," my mother added, bending to untangle a string of Christmas lights.

"I think she's really pretty," I said.

"She never wears makeup."

"That's why she's pretty."

"I think she's plain."

"Okay, Diana." I went back to cutting the snowflakes. It surprised me that, after all these years in Topsfield, my mother didn't have an urge to befriend anyone on our street. I think it was her feeling of inferiority that held her back, her own prejudices against these white-collar neighbors. Like most of her evasions, in the end she was only hurting herself.

"What, I can't have an opinion? That's all you girls do is talk about people. Who has holes in their clothes. Who doesn't straighten their hair."

"Wonder where we learned that from," Sofia said, sifting through the box of decorations.

"Go upstairs if you don't want to hear my opinions."

Sofia laughed. "Are you sending us to our rooms?"

"I don't know what you guys stayed home for. If you were just going to be starting fights."

"That's because you can't argue for five seconds without freaking out." Sofia tossed a candle in the cardboard box.

"Oh my God. Stop it. The two of you," I said.

"I don't know how anyone can stand you," Sofia said to my mother, her voice breaking a little.

I was surprised she was getting so upset.

"Yeah, go cry about it," my mother said. "Little baby."

Sofia marched upstairs, trying to be defiant, but looking silly with the big blanket wrapped around her. I wished I could reverse the minutes—take back the nice thing I'd said about Carol.

Sofia and my mother made up, like they always did. Around lunchtime, Lia called the house, asking my mother to bring one of her notebooks to the school—she'd left it on her nightstand and there was an important assignment inside. To my surprise, my mother agreed. Maybe it felt good to be needed. I went with her for the ride, my slippered feet perched on the dashboard while I picked at a blueberry muffin, ducking whenever another mother drove past.

We weren't allowed to listen to music when my mother was driving. When she parked and trailed to the front doors of the building, I turned the volume on high. From the corner of my eye, I saw her figure reemerging from the double doors. But the figure faltered, skidded, and landed on a patch of ice, flat on her palms and knees. It took me a few seconds to react, my mother on the ground, in pain. I was halfway out of the car, when I saw a woman dashing in my mother's direction. Natasha.

My mother waved a hand to show that she was okay, but she struggled to stand. Natasha was bending down to help when I noticed a circle of ninth-grade girls pointing and laughing from several feet away. I was suddenly aware of my body, my pulse quickening, mashed blueberry muffin sitting in my mouth. How was my mother going to get over this? Did people know she was my mother?

Natasha started yelling. "You think that's funny, you little monsters? Where were you raised? A fucking barn?"

I'd never heard Natasha raise her voice, never heard her swear.

The head of the pack, a blonde, sank into one hip. "I'm telling my mom."

"Yeah, you tell her. You tell her exactly what happened." For a moment, she reminded me of Debbie.

Natasha helped my mother off the ground and led her inside, where, I found out later, she persuaded the principal to suspend the girls. My mother told me this while she iced her knees in the kitchen. "They got what they deserved. Imagine that? Laughing at a lady when she falls? I bet their mothers are mortified. I bet they'll come to this house with flowers."

"I'm shocked Natasha said those things."

My mother studied her nails, started picking. "She's okay. I never really cared for her, but that was a nice thing to do."

My mother and Natasha didn't become friends after that, but my mother stopped talking badly about her. She told me to say hello for her whenever I went to Vera's. She waved when she saw Natasha at the mailbox, smiling guardedly. These small gestures meant a lot coming from her, and I think Natasha knew this, just as she knew not to push for friendship or neighborly intimacy. The occasional greeting, the odd small talk, was enough.

20

On warm nights, I sat by the giant pit next door, legs dangling over the edge while the gravel pricked my thighs. At sunset hour, I liked to go down there to think and to dream and be alone. No one would look for me there. Behind me, the windows of the house blinked when figures passed. I thought of the running pipes and buzzing lights, water heaters and vents, until the house became a living thing, and I felt sad knowing the five of us would not always be a part of it. Sometimes, I thought about Beans down in the pit, imagined his twisted limbs sinking into the mud, his eyes bulging, his drenched hair spiking outward. How my father might have felt when he found him.

My mother had gotten in the habit of divulging my father's miserable history. She told me about the aftermath of his father's death—how, when my father was ten and his father buried, he sat on the front porch with his ball and street hockey stick, expecting the black Oldsmobile to pull into the driveway. He did this daily, after school, waiting for his dead dad to come home.

My father had a scar, a straight dash across his left cheek that shone blunt and bright against his dark skin. He never told us the full story, only alluded to getting in a fistfight with his younger brother, something to do with a fireplace. My father smacked his face on stone during the fight. There was a lot of tension in my father's family, a lot of anger. He kept us at a distance from them. And I suspect this tension is what fueled his desire to leave Everett in the first place. He wasn't tied to the place the way my mother was.

She reminded me that he was one of three boys, the middle child, but the only one my grandmother chose not to send to college because she couldn't afford it. The only one with crooked teeth. My mother once pointed to the photograph of my father as a high school senior on my grandmother's mantelpiece—the sleeves of his hand-me-down suit barely reaching the knobs of his wrists. "Should've seen his pants that day," she said. "Up to his ankles." My mother taught me everything I knew about my father.

I knew it was wrong to measure my parents' lacks and losses, but it's something I did often. I tried to decide which of them was the stronger person. To me, the answer was never obvious, ever changing, and this lack of certainty made me uneasy. I believed it was important for me to know which of them I should turn to, a strategy of survival.

He was out drinking in Cambridge one Friday evening, entertaining his clients and meeting with realtors, and I was the only one at home with my mother. I had to be responsible, alert to her sadness. Lia and Sofia were staying at friends' houses. If left alone, she'd just drug herself to sleep.

My father called to check in, which was rare on nights when he had to work, and my mother answered the phone with the fragile voice of an invalid. "Just sitting here," she said, hoping to evoke sympathy. The call lasted less than a minute.

"What did he say?" I asked, sliding onto the couch.

"Nothing."

Some of the older neighbors were out in their yards, laughing and clinking their glasses. They had their grills going. The scent of sweet peppers and onions was traveling through our screens. It was chilly with the breeze coming in, the water glass cool in my hands. My mother was warm. I could sit beside her, allow the heat of her skin to radiate, but it had been years since I'd sat that close to her.

"Do you know where he is?"

"Somewhere with Doherty and the others."

William Doherty had gone to high school with my parents, and my mother had spent the last twenty years trying to get rid of him. She thought William was a sleazeball who cheated on his wife and barely talked to his kids, who loved dragging my father down the coast for fishing trips. A *butta' gazz'* she used to call him, a butchering of some Italian phrase that meant "annoying idiot."

"When I was your age, I was friends with everyone—the popular kids, the nerds, even the weird people," my mother said. "Ivy Bergeron never washed her clothes—always had pen marks and face makeup on her neckline. I still sat with her on the bus. But not William Doherty. Used to make me sick to my stomach with his dirty jokes. Tactless. Crude. That's what he is." She complained that my father was naive.

She sucked air through her teeth, ran her hand from her wrist to her elbow. I refrained from asking her what was wrong.

"My arm is numb," she said, lifting her arm to show me. "I can't feel it."

Why was she cringing at the touch if she couldn't feel anything? It was better not to ask. "Since when?"

"Since I woke up." Her lips turned upward—she couldn't help but laugh at her own dramatics. She must have realized I wasn't going to bite because she changed the subject completely. "We were supposed to pick out pictures tonight for the upstairs hall. He was going to drive me to one of the antique places in Newburyport. Maybe have dinner on the water."

It was only then that I noticed our pet guinea pig resting on her chest, below her chin.

Chip stretched his body and sniffed, scurried down the length of my mother. She let him hop off to explore.

"Did he forget?" I asked. "Did you remind him?"

She raked her fingers through her hair. There was a hole in the armpit of her nightgown.

"Did you pick a fight?"

"How could I have started a fight with him, Anna? I've been sitting right here all day. You and your sisters. Always blaming shit on me."

The guinea pig rose on his hind legs to gnaw at my mother's iced-coffee cup. "You want some coffee, Pig?" She bent the straw toward his tiny oval-shaped mouth despite the fact that she was allergic to him.

"Ew, Mom. You're sharing a straw with a rodent."

Far off, an engine revved. The sound grew closer, beams of light breaking through the windows. It was only the neighbors' kids.

"Will you call him?" my mother asked.

"I don't want to."

She narrowed her eyes to make me feel stupid—a gesture I later perfected and deployed to make her feel the same.

"I feel bad," I said.

"You feel bad for your father getting drunk until three in the morning, but you don't feel bad for me?"

"I do feel bad for you."

"He's driving, you know, even when he's drinking."

I did know, but I tried not to think about it. Occasionally, after happy hours with his clients, my father took us to the movies in the Chevy. He'd teeter over the yellow line, near the curb, back to the yellow line. With my sisters in the truck, I'd sit in the middle seat, alert, fingers crossed so tight they throbbed. *Please don't let anything bad happen.* I'd call his name when he went too fast, or else my mother would. I'd dip low in my seat while my sisters slept with their heads against the windows, fluorescent green earbuds in their ears.

When I didn't respond, my mother scoffed.

"Fine," she said. "We'll wait until his truck is wrapped around a tree."

Please don't let anything bad happen. I wanted my mother to ask why I was crossing my fingers, for her to get a sense of how much I worried. But she didn't see.

Alone in my room, I recounted the things I wished I'd said to my mother, to my sisters, to my father. Often, I could barely sleep, haunted by images of my father with a bleeding face. My mother in her own room, waiting, in bed with her crossword puzzles. Maybe she was watching the clock radio on my father's nightstand. We were the same—fighting off sleep until our pink eyes filled with tears, nodding off until we woke to rooms too warm and too bright, not comprehending why the lights were on, waiting for everyone to come home.

I woke to a shout and the rush of broken glass, my father vomiting in the kitchen sink. There was another crash. He threw up again and collapsed on the floor. The clock on my bedside read 1:42 a.m.

It was becoming an unwelcome familiarity. The front door swinging, banging into the foyer wall, its floral wreath falling with a thud. I could chart his whereabouts by his uneven steps. Sometimes, I predicted the sounds, waking moments before my father stepped into the house. I'd sit up, body swaying with the weight of sleep, waiting for him to wake me from my trance.

My mother made her way down the stairs, huffing when she reached the landing. Their whispers echoed from the kitchen.

"Get up," I heard her say.

The rise and fall of his obscure sounds.

"Get up! Do you know what time it is?"

A clatter of pots and pans, more throwing up.

"Yeah, laugh now, Vin," she said. "Laugh now because maybe you'll wake up tomorrow and I won't be here."

"That—" He paused to laugh. "Would be something, Dee." I waited for my mother to respond, but there was only silence.

"You're pathetic."

"I know." A large huffing sound from my father. "I'm the pathetic one."

As she approached the stairs, I slid into the shadows. It was my mother I hated in that moment. I didn't understand how she could be so passive, how she could accept this from my father.

I waited for him to move to the living room—to hear his deep flop onto the couch. I crept downstairs, feeling my way through the dark. There was a gentle creaking throughout the house. I found him lying facedown, his dress shoes pressed into the leather. Afraid someone might hurt themselves on the shards of glass, I cleaned up the mess in the kitchen. I pulled a folded blanket out from the cedar chest, considered shaking it out and spreading it evenly across my snoring father. When I reached him, I only placed it flat and compact on his shoulders.

"I'm sorry, Dee," he said into the pillow, his eyes closed.

When morning came, a milky fog lifted off the grass. Sprinklers ticked on the lawn. I was resting in bed when there was a knock on the doorframe. My father poked his head into my room, fresh-faced, a backward cap sweeping the black hair from his temples. One of his pant legs was tucked into his sock.

"Coffee's in the fridge, hon."

I dropped my head onto the pillow, exhausted.

"I got everything bagels, blueberry. Onion for your mother."

"Apology bagels," I muttered.

I lay on my back, sun-huddled, with the light sprayed across my eyes, squinting at the flints of dust and fiber that swam in the air. I'd been a fool, awake with worry, only to be greeted in the morning by a different man—someone who was calm and controlled—as if I'd invented the entire episode. I could never bring myself to tell him what I'd seen the night before, face against the leather, drooling. I didn't want to shame him, make him feel underappreciated.

A large crow swooped past my window and darkened the room.

"Let's go to the beach," he said, eyes bright. "Maybe we can rent a Jet Ski and ride out from Boston Harbor." He glanced out the window. "Have a picnic on a sandbar. It's a good day for it."

"Really?" We hadn't been anywhere that summer. I pictured the five of us sitting on the sand in our bathing suits and life jackets, slapping horseflies off our legs. My mother would toss diced tomatoes to the seagulls.

Waiting for my sisters to come home, I watched my father skim tree pollen off the pool water. I sat on a green-and-white lounge chair by the deep end, forced my arms onto the sun-scorched plastic, to see how long I could keep them there.

He was at the pool's edge in his wrinkled button-down and khaki shorts. Tufts of hair sprouted from the collar of his pale blue shirt, patchy with sweat.

"Dad?" I was louder than I meant to be, startling him. One of his knees bent and he almost slipped in the water. I laughed. "Are you still going to build that pizza oven back here?"

"You bet. Just have to find the time."

In the old, tiny backyard, my father had managed to build a two-story tree house, complete with lavender curtains and flower boxes beneath the windows. My mother told us stories about children falling from them, breaking their bones, and the older I got, the more afraid I was to go up there.

"How are you going to do it?" I asked. "The pizza oven."

"Have to design it first. Then lay the bricks with mortar."

"Can I help you when you start?"

"Sure thing." He picked up the giant bag of chemicals, sprinkling them evenly around the kidney-shaped pool. He filled his mouth with air so his upper lip puffed out, his concentrated look. I puffed my lip out, too, to see what it felt like.

When my sisters returned, my father was busy with one of his work projects, asking us to stand by for a few hours. Lia, Sofia, and I made smoothies, diced up strawberries and bananas and tossed them in the blender. We took our frothy pink drinks to the front porch and sat there with our beach bags at our feet. I wished I'd taken my time drinking mine, because now the moment felt far away, like it'd never happened. The hours ticked by and everyone was in a bad mood.

"I guess we're not going," Sofia mumbled, her lips squashed against her knees.

"Just give it a few more minutes, Soph."

She played with her toe ring, twisting it. Her bare feet were outlined with tan marks from the straps of her summer sandals. She was ten and spent most of her time outside, taking long walks down the trails in the woods, coming back with leaves and flowers, collections of heart-shaped rocks for our mother. At thirteen, I felt light-years away from that.

"This is so lame," Lia said. The hose lay at the bottom of the steps, a skin of mulch on the green casing. She picked it up with two fingers and it bubbled at the mouth, letting out its warm, metallic smell. "We're waiting around like idiots."

"I bet he's almost done," I said.

"I'm calling Rachel."

"He's going to be sad if you leave, Lia."

"Like I care."

There was a brutal thud when a bird flew into the front window. The hydrangea bush shook when the bird broke its fall, and the three of us stared open-mouthed, stunned.

Lia brushed off her shorts and walked into the house.

I placed my palms on the cool concrete, keeping them there until I couldn't feel the difference. We didn't go to the beach that day.

PART III

Everett, Massachusetts

1979

Every year, when summer rolls around, he drops her off at her cousins' with a small orange suitcase and a wad of cash, says he'll see her in September. She wakes to the same image each day: Auntie Pina sitting on the couch in her Minnie Mouse nightgown, watching her soaps and eating a bowl of pasta e fagioli. They don't talk about why she's there. Dee and Julia spend most of their time outside, riding bikes and blowing bubbles, excluding Charles when they make trips to the corner store for candy cigarettes. A water hose leaks and builds a stream, and they construct boats out of leaves, send them sailing. A stray kitten mews and paws, rolls onto its back for rubs. Every few hours, the television runs static and the girls can hear Auntie Pina hollering from the street.

One afternoon, Auntie Pina catches them on the phone, asking the operator for the Danvers State Hospital. She rips the phone from Dee's hand, practically spitting, "Don't you think that's the first place we called?"

In September, like clockwork, her father raps on the front door, arriving to bring her home.

21

I have a question," Vera said, running a bookmark from my pulse point to my elbow. "Am I your only friend? It's okay if I am," she added, a cruelty in her voice that only I could detect.

It was the summer I turned fifteen. Vera and I spent our days in her backyard, tanning and dashing through the sprinklers with our clothes on. We tore open fresh lemons, dripped the juice in our hair. Lying head to toe on the hammock with a red boom box nestled in the grass, we dried out in the sun, our limbs buzzing with excitement, shirts glued to our skin.

"You're not." I untwisted the strings of my bikini top. "I have friends from other towns. Somerville and places around there. Because of my dad's work. And where we used to live."

She continued to stroke my arm. Vera liked to cling and cuddle, something I was unused to, though I did like the tickling, aching feeling, both wanting it to last and wanting to tear away.

Her own arms were decked out in beaded bracelets made by her mother—hues of tangerine and turquoise. A heap of six slid down her left forearm. Her left hand was also taken over by jewelry, sterling silver wrapped around every finger, her right side completely bare. "I guess I like being a little off-balance," she once said. I envied that she had an answer for everything, that she knew herself so well, even at sixteen.

"So, their parents work for your dad?" she asked. "What are their names?"

I recited the first names that came to mind. "Elizabeth, Heather, Mary . . ." Two were characters in a book I was reading, the other the daughter of our neighbor in the old house.

"Interesting," Vera said, her tone disbelieving. She twisted her sun-splashed curls to the top of her head and let them fall, looking like her mother. She let out a deep breath. "I just love the summer."

As we grew older, Vera often sat me down for "talks" about how to better myself, though these were not talks so much as seminars, one-sided monologues. Vera seemed to believe she was an expert on the subject of me. "You're fragile, Anna," she once said. "It's like you need to be taken care of. I feel responsible for you. And that's a lot for me."

Funny, coming from a girl who could lie for hours with her head in her mother's lap, dozing while her mother's fingers combed through her hair. I despised this trait in Vera, her mix of interest and mockery, of bossiness and vulnerability. I'd identified her condescension long ago and expected this kind of manipulation, perhaps even sought it. I think Vera, being an only child, was sometimes envious of my sisters and the bond we shared, the fact that we would never really be alone. It was maddening—the way she inserted herself in any sibling squab-

ble, taking the side of my sisters. Didn't she know she was supposed to remain loyal to me? "I think Lia's right on this one,"
she'd say, gesturing toward Lia with a half-eaten sandwich, or,
"Sofia kind of has a point." She loved to implant herself in the
middle of everything, thereby pushing me out of the circle. And
she was bringing out the worst in Lia, trying to mold my sister
into a mini version of her. Lia had started adopting Vera's mannerisms, like the constant hair touching, even her laugh. I wholly
expected them to merge into the same person.

Vera got her driver's license that summer. We were sitting in her
Jeep one afternoon, in the parking lot of the soccer field. "I have
an idea," she said, pausing to take a drag of her cigarette, a new
habit I'd chosen to ignore. "Let's give ourselves tattoos."

She was holding a purple lighter and a rusting smiley-face
key chain. The eyes and mouth were carved out.

"With those?"

"We heat up the key chain with the lighter and then we put
it to our skin, here." She pointed to her inner wrist. "We'll do it
quick. It won't hurt that bad. And it will be faint. Like a scar."

"Does it have to be a smiley face?"

She popped open the glove box, sifted through it. "It'll have
to work. It's all I have." She stretched the items toward me. "You
first. I have to finish this." She held up her cigarette. "Oh, come
on," she said, when I didn't immediately react.

I took the objects from Vera's hand. I didn't want to be the one to say no. And she was probably right. It couldn't be that painful. Not any more painful than a real tattoo.

I spent a good minute heating up the underside of the key chain, making sure I got the edges, watching the flame bend and dance. I took a deep breath, pressed the metal to my skin, and screamed, hurling the thing to the floor.

"Oh, fuck," I heard Vera say. She clapped her hand over her mouth.

I cradled mine in my lap, trying not to touch the searing skin. I lifted my wrist and blew. It felt a little better. "Jesus." Once I'd managed the pain, I held out the lighter and key chain. She didn't move to take it. "Vera."

"No way, dude."

"You're not going to do it?"

"Look at that thing!" She pointed to my wrist, at the distorted, simmering smile. It was so ugly.

I glared at her fingers wrapped around the cigarette, the chipped nails, lime green. I should have known she'd back out. When I came home that night, my mother was almost brought to tears. "Who the hell's going to date you? A friggin' smiley-face blister on your wrist!"

My fears about Lia and Vera were beginning to play out. Toward the end of that summer, Lia was spending more time across the street at Vera's, without me, making me feel invasive when I tried to join in, driving me deeper into a hollow of exclusion. I

was sure they were growing bored of me and feared I was holding them back in some way. That was the year they both decided
they weren't going to eat meat anymore. Lia watched with
repugnance at the table when the rest of us cut into our veal
cutlets. She, too, started smoking cigarettes, spraying herself relentlessly with perfume, and eating mints, barely masking the
smell.

I tried to include myself in their outings, like when they hung
out in the parking lot of the new Dunkin' Donuts—one of the
only commercial buildings for miles—its pink neon blinking
against the pine trees and dust roads. One afternoon, I stood
with Vera and Lia against the chain-link fence, my bare legs itching in the dry grass. Clouds yawned overhead, pulling us into
gray. We tugged our sleeves over our palms, cradled our hands,
inhaled the honeyed trace of garbage from the dumpsters.

There was a young couple sitting at an outdoor table. The
man read a newspaper while the woman fished in her bag and
pulled out a pink-frosted doughnut. When she took a bite, a
clump of frosting fell to her lap. Without looking up from his
paper, the man used his finger to reach over, dab the frosting up,
and press it onto his tongue. It disgusted and pleased me at the
same time. I was excited for that kind of intimacy, one day.

"Stop being a creep," Lia said, catching me.

She was increasingly hostile, quick to insult me. At school,
she'd become known for her promiscuousness, though I wasn't
sure she'd had sex. I often passed her at the lockers, a group of
boys convened around her, flirting. When she caught my eye,

she'd look the other way. I'd breeze past her without acknowledgment, so as not to inflict shame—on her, on me.

I pretended it was normal when Vera pulled a pack of Marlboro Lights from her canvas bag. It took her a few tries to light a cigarette before she passed the pack to Lia. The hot, orange tip puckered between her acrylic nails, this time electric blue. Neither of them offered me a drag, though I would have taken it. I was sick of watching them, like my own experiences were less important than theirs. They both wore too much makeup, circling their eyes twice with charcoal liner. Their shirts were so tight the indents of their belly buttons showed through.

I avoided my sister's eyes when she ashed with the flick of a wrist, her arm falling naturally to her side. I could feel her looking at me.

The two of them perked up when a group of men assembled across the parking lot. They were older, construction workers, not the sort of men that teenage girls typically swooned over. Lia and Vera were both attracted to the grungy type—sweat-marked baseball caps and greasy hair, grimy blue jeans dappled with stains.

The men relaxed their arms over the beds of their trucks, yelling out to each other. Coffee brimmed their styrofoam cups, tilted and splashed over the rims. They discarded the lids in the messy truck beds, spat dip on the pavement. Their hands were big and tan and dotted with plaster. I watched them reaching for their Red Sox caps, grazing them across rumpled hair, popping them back on. One of the men rolled a straw wrapper between his fingers, eyeing my sister. He winked, then he drew his wet tongue the length of his bottom lip. A little noise came from Lia's throat that only I could hear.

Vera jabbed my sister. "Look at you," she said, proud.

"I don't get it," I said. He had to have been thirty, twice her age, though this didn't concern me for reasons it should have.

"I think they're sexy," Lia said, biting the tip of her straw.

"They're, like, gross. They're old. They have beer guts."

"Don't be such a snob," said Vera.

"As if you'd actually hook up with a guy like that."

"I'm not picky," Lia said. "I want a man who knows what he's doing. Rough with scruff and in the buff."

She didn't have any idea what she was saying.

"That one's staring at you, Anna," Vera said, wiggling her hips.

I twisted around, locked eyes with another worker, a redhead. I snapped back around, like a frightened animal.

"Well, not anymore he isn't," my sister said.

"Tell me when he stops looking," I said.

"He *stopped*. Oh my God," Vera said. "Look how red she is."

Vera and Lia were smiling at me, cheeks puffing out, and then they erupted with laughter. They were laughing for attention, collapsing into each other, Vera's head on Lia's shoulder. I tightened my fingers around the rusted links of the fence.

"Those men are like forty," I said. "I don't want them looking at me."

Lia smirked. "Better get used to it." Maybe it was the piercing green eyes—the glasses were gone, replaced by contacts—or the smattering of moles on her face, like someone had flicked a paintbrush over it, but there was something off-putting in Lia's resting expression. It made me think something bad would come her way.

And Vera. I was hopelessly, irrevocably, jealous of her. Sometimes I caught myself glaring at her so deeply, I was shocked neither of them had called me out. "Look at my little frecklies," she'd said that afternoon, inspecting the scattering of new freckles on her nose in her compact mirror. *You mean sunspots*, I wanted to say.

I brushed away the hair that clung to my arms like spiderwebs, glanced down at my gangling figure. I'd spent most of my time locked away indoors with books and music, the fan on high. I lay on the bed in my underwear, basking in the flutter of papers, trying to ignore Lia and Vera's new friendship.

"Should we head back?" Lia asked, stubbing out her cigarette.

The men gathered into their trucks, roaring the engines. When they drove off, we tossed our coffees in the dumpster. I made Lia wait until the intersection was completely clear before we crossed.

On a muggy night that August, after everyone had gone to bed, I woke to pale orbs of light shining through my curtains, the slamming of a car door. If I hadn't known he was asleep down the hall, I would have thought it was my father coming home.

I sat up in the buzzing silence, not sure if I'd dreamt it. Then I heard the sounds of someone in the mudroom, bumping into things, slipping off their shoes, climbing unbalanced up the stairs. They were the footsteps of someone trying to be discreet.

There was a knock on my door. Then it cracked it open. "Anna?"

Lia kept her head down as she circled my bed, lifting the white sheets and sliding beneath them. I figured she'd been drinking because it was unlike her, at this age, to sleep in my bed, to seek me out for comfort. Her jeans were damp, the bottoms crusted in sand, and her hair was soft and wind-whipped. She smelled like the ocean. I tried to act like her climbing into my bed was normal, something we did as sisters.

"He took me to his house in Gloucester," she said, after a few soft breaths. "Well, the beach. His parents don't know about me." I didn't know who she was referring to, and I got the sense that she didn't want me to know. She nodded when I asked if they'd slept together.

"Did you want to?"

"I don't know."

"Did it hurt?"

She pulled her knees up, picked at a thread on my pillowcase. I could hear her breaths quickening between tears. I didn't say another word, just placed my hand on her knee as her body shook, not knowing what else to do. I knew that if it were the other way around, Lia would know. I tried to ignore the tiny, gnawing feeling in me that was jealous it'd happened to her first, that she was doing everything before me, even if she didn't want to.

The next morning, her side of the bed was empty. Pebbles and sand were leftover like cracker crumbs, a sister-shaped dent in the sheets. I remembered Lia's head resting on my shoulder in the night, like when we were kids. We never spoke of it again.

22

For a long time, they fight behind Vera's closed door. I drift off to her crying, and when I wake the next morning, they're both gone. I spend the day on the couch, ready to talk when she comes home, prepared to do anything, prepared to beg. As evening advances, the living room grays. I'm alone and panicked by the seep of night, but I don't turn on the lights.

Please don't let anything bad happen.

What happens when you're the one who does the bad thing?

I don't hear Vera when she finally comes through the door, don't notice her standing in the center of the room like a ghost, her long hair curtaining her face. The lights flash on, cutting the dark. Her eyes are sunken and black with makeup. Every word is a whisper except for the last: "I don't even know what to say to you."

"I'm disgusted with myself," I say. "You have every right to hate me."

"I *do* hate you. You've ruined everything." She wipes her nose with her sleeve and starts crying, hard, how I imagine most of her day was spent.

"Are you and Jonathan—"

"We're done."

"I'm sorry, Vera."

"Please. This is exactly what you wanted."

I stare down at my wrist, run my fingers over the faint scar. I can't look at her. I feel like an idiot.

"What did I ever do to you?"

"I don't know what's wrong with me."

"This isn't new, Anna. You've always been this way. Controlling, jealous. A victim."

My voice won't rise above a whisper. "He's a horrible person and you can't see it—"

"No. You're the horrible person. Look at your life."

I want her to stop. I need her to.

"Look at what you're doing to your own family. Oh, give me a break with the tears, Anna. You don't get to be sad."

My head is pounding. I feel sick.

"I just don't understand this. I've always been here for you." It comes out as a question.

"You have. Vera, I'm sorry." I try my hardest not to cry, but faced with losing her, with losing the last good thing, I find it impossible.

I flinch at the memory of his fingers in my hair, his pawing at me from above, the imposing pluck of his kissing. It sends a wave through my stomach. I don't recognize the girl in this scene looping in my mind. "I know this sounds pathetic—I didn't mean it the way you think I did. I don't know why I did it . . . why I do these things."

Vera slaps a hand over her eyes. I'm prepared for her to really lose it, but then her face softens. To my surprise, she comes to sit next to me. There's a quick knock on the wall.

"Not now, Nathaniel," she says. I don't know if I'm allowed to laugh. She turns more serious. "Let's call, Anna. I'll do it with you." She picks up my phone and holds it out to me.

"Why are you being nice?"

She relaxes her shoulders. She looks exhausted. "Because I know this doesn't have to do with me. At least, I don't think it does." She makes a move like she's shaking something off. "Come on. We'll find out from Sofia."

I gently push the phone in her direction. "Will you do it?"

23

o you girls want to play a joke on your father?" my mother asked one afternoon, a warm day on the edge of summer and fall. It was the start of my junior year. We were snacking at the kitchen table and organizing our school binders. I looked up from my pile of folders, not sure I'd heard her right.

"What kind of joke?" Sofia asked.

"Just a little one," my mother said, pinching the air with her fingers. "Call and tell him you don't know where I am. I went out when you came home from school and I never came back." She lifted a peanut butter–coated knife, licked the blade.

"That's stupid," Lia said, reaching for the burning candle on the table. She dipped her fingers in the pool of wax, careful not to touch the flame. It hardened on her fingers and she peeled it off, orange clusters snowing on the table. I waited for my mother to yell at her, but she was too focused on her little joke.

"Sofia will do it," she said, eyeing my sister.

"That's mean," Sofia said. "Why do you want to make him worry?"

She laughed, peanut butter clinging to the roof of her mouth. I could see the bits of silver drilled into every one of her molars. "It's funny," she said.

"What would you want me to say?" Sofia asked.

"That I went to the store after school and you're worried because I'm not home yet."

"That's messed up," Lia said, too confident this time. "Don't do it, Sofia."

"Stop destroying my candle," my mother said without looking at her.

"You're just going to piss him off," Lia added. Again, she dipped her fingers into the warm wax.

My mother was starting to turn red. "What'd I just say?"

Lia gave no indication that she'd heard my mother, sank her fingers deeper.

"That's it." In one motion, my mother rose from her chair, grabbed Lia's book bag, and whipped it across the table, aiming for her head. The bag was empty but it was loud when it hit her. Lia shot up, her hair a snarled web in front of her eyes. She was blinking wildly, stunned, confused. I was half standing, my bottom barely touching the chair. Sofia shrouded beside Lia, fingers stuffed in her mouth, a little girl again.

"You're a psycho," Lia eventually screamed. "Fucking *tapped*." She went to her room and when she slammed her door, the little bird chime that hung on the knob clanged hard against the wood.

"She's a little witch," my mother said. "If I ever talked to my mother that way . . ."

"You threw a backpack at her head," I said.

"I could have done a lot worse."

Sofia and I knew better than to speak. My mother reached for the candle and dragged it close to her. Then she dipped her own fingers inside.

That fall, I found a receipt in the center console of my father's truck for expensive dishware from a housing store that never made it to our cabinets. I went to Lia's room late one night, the receipt pinched in my fist. She wasn't even surprised. She shuffled through the top drawer of her bureau and revealed the write-up for a washing machine repair at a different address. She'd spotted the paper a week earlier in the laundry room, peeping out from the pocket of his jeans.

Looking back, I think we'd expected it. There was the fact of our mother, who was enough to drive any man crazy, and the fact that women had always been attracted to our father. It wasn't difficult to understand why. They were drawn to his restraint, his mysteriousness; his presumed thoughtfulness. I'd seen them flirting with him at school functions over the years, and I suspected he'd eventually give in to one of them. What most troubled me was the fact that I could not blame him, though I was surprised by how little care he took to hide his infidelity. It didn't seem impossible to me that a good person could be led astray. In the end, Lia and I agreed not to tell Sofia, to wait for more signs.

He began treating my mother with a new kindness, bringing lunch home to her during his workday, unprompted. She didn't question it, like I thought she would. For a brief, beautiful time, she seemed somewhat normal. On weekends, she woke early and returned with treats for the four of us—cinnamon sugar doughnuts from the farmers' market, blueberry and pumpkin pies, fresh cartons of apple cider. She went for daily walks, coming back with thick twigs that we later spray-painted gold and arranged in vases. She took care of herself, carrying a gallon water bottle beneath her arm everywhere she went, making healthy meals—arugula and orange salads that shone with olive oil. She was kind and didn't lose her temper. She knew nothing about my father's betrayal.

The three of us were walking home from the bus stop one afternoon, when we noticed his Chevy parked in the driveway earlier than usual. When we stepped into the house, something felt changed. The hall was dark with the sun setting behind a tuft of white in the sky. Water boiled in the kitchen. Walking through the hall, we were enveloped by the familiar scents of tomato, basil, and garlic. We rounded the corner and saw the island was covered in flour and egg wash. Our father stood goofily by the stove in a giant chef hat that was creased from being stuffed in a drawer. Our mother was giddy, arranging meats and cheeses on a crystal platter, anticipating our delight. Behind me, the table was papered with blueprints and notepads. My father must have worked from home.

"Gnocchis!" Sofia shouted. "You should have waited!" She loved pressing grooves into the potato dough.

"There's a whole other batch," my father said, pointing with his shoulder to a fresh mound.

Sofia and Lia got to work, pulling clumps from the dough, rolling them into pipes. I stood back, eyeing him. I couldn't remember the last time he'd made a meal at home, and I wondered what it meant.

"Your father wanted to surprise you," said my mother.

"Mama's making antipasti."

"What's the occasion?" Lia asked.

"Anna, come look what your father bought me." I followed her gesture to the window, to the stone object in the center of the grass. "It's a birdbath," she said.

"For the crazy bird lady," my father added.

"Ew, Dad. She already has, like, three," I said.

"The others got knocked down by all the snow last winter."

I felt bad for my mother, a little angry at my father, whose good mood was untrustworthy. I suspected it was brought on by someone else, and I didn't like that he was tricking our mother this way, letting her think everything was normal, or worse, getting better.

She rubbed her hand up and down my father's arm. "Hey, Soph," she said. "Get the mortadella out of the fridge?"

Sofia laughed in a mean way. "Why are you saying it like that? With that accent?"

"That's how you say it."

"It's how the *Italians* say it."

"I *am* Italian!"

"Yeah, but not really," Sofia said. "You're not *from* there."

"My mother's from there! I'm Italian. Vin, tell her. I'm Italian on all sides!"

I was making swirls on the counter when my father's phone vibrated next to me. I glimpsed at the screen before he noticed.

Hi Vincent, read the text.

I laughed, grossed out. No one called my father Vincent. "Dad, who's Trisha?"

The phone buzzed a second time. *Cab or chianti tonight? Heading to the store.*

It dawned on me slowly, then stung like a slap. I knew who Trisha was. This woman had been to the house before with a stack of checks for my father to sign. It was raining. She sat opposite my father, brown-black ringlets dripping onto the table, her face pale and clear. She was quick too. Unafraid to make fun of my father for his illegible signature, for his old-man reading glasses. She was too pleasant to my mother, complimenting the house, taking a cup of tea when my mother offered it, effusive in her gratitude.

My hands were trembling, sweating. I wanted to throw the phone across the room.

My father snatched it. "Work stuff," he said.

I was surprised to see my mother already frowning, her mind probably ticking through the possibilities of what I had seen. She wasn't stupid; she'd noticed my reaction. She held on to her coffee cup, not moving a finger. I wondered if, like Lia and me, she thought it was inevitable.

~

Two days later, a Friday, I slept through my alarm. Waking late had triggered the feeling that something was wrong. Traipsing from my room wearing a blanket like a shawl, I did the rounds to make sure everyone was okay. In the big bathroom, a blow dryer whirred to life. Lia fussed with her hair while Sofia slept standing up, hands draped beneath the warm running faucet. Through the big window, the rain-flattened lawn lay motionless beneath the darkening sky, except for a pair of napkins, starkly white, which ambled down the sidewalk.

I found my mother in the kitchen wearing yesterday's clothes. The checkered imprint of a placemat marked her cheek.

Mom, check. Sisters, check. We're all here.

"I just woke up," I announced, as if it were someone else's fault. I placed the rolled-up blanket on the countertop, reached a hand in the open box of Froot Loops.

My mother rested her head in her arms.

"Why are you up?" I asked her, crunching on dry cereal.

"Your father didn't come home last night. I've been up all hours. Head's pounding." She looked at the garage door, at the wall clock, back at the door.

"Have you called him?" I asked.

"Obviously." She brought a hand up, shielding herself from my question.

I tried to think of another explanation, but Trisha was the first to come to my mind. Was she out drinking with him? Lying in bed with him? Was he using her shower or frying eggs in her kitchen?

"His phone is going straight to voicemail." She took a swig from her coffee mug, set it down, hard, on the table. She flexed her fingers. Their period of getting along was over now. My mother's anxieties returned.

"This is it, Anna," she said. "Get ready."

"Stop."

She was turning wild, spinning from lack of sleep and worry. She went to the sink to wash out her cup. "I don't know what to do. Call the police? Hospitals? I don't know." She paced out of the room.

I pressed my palms on the granite, repeatedly telling myself he was on his way home. He was probably drumming his fingers on the steering wheel, singing to the radio, on his way up the hill.

"Oh, you've got to be friggin' kidding me," she called from the foyer.

My stomach dropped.

"Come on, everybody! Come downstairs!" She was shouting with a strange half-happy kind of rage.

My sisters came to the upstairs banister, toothbrushes hanging from their mouths.

"Come see what your father does to me!"

I was afraid, slow to turn the corner. From her tone, I could sense my father was in a state he wouldn't want me to see, one I probably didn't want to see either. I wanted to stay in the house but my sisters were already gathering by the foyer windows.

She pulled back the curtain with one tentative finger. "This is just great." She laughed to herself. "Anyone have a camera?"

When she opened the front door, I saw only white. A dense fog had crept in, clouding everything but the glow of the streetlamps. She opened the door wider, letting drizzle hit my cheeks.

I caught sight of him in the front seat of his Chevy, one leg hanging out the door, the other bent at the steering wheel. There was the faint *bing*ing of an alarm from inside the truck. Napkins and loose papers had blown out the open door. His mouth hung gaping while his head dangled onto one shoulder. By the looks of it, he'd fallen asleep while getting out of his truck.

"Mom, go help him," Sofia said, not moving her eyes from my father. They were big and red with fear. The look on her face brought it back to me—the first time I'd seen him so altered. I hadn't wanted this sadness to touch Sofia.

"Why should I help him?" my mother asked.

"He's just really tired from working, Soph," Lia said.

"The whole neighborhood's probably seen him. Hey, Vin! Your kids are wondering why you're sleeping outside," she yelled, basting him in guilt. But he was someplace else, unable to hear. His foot moved an inch or two down the pavement.

"Dumbass."

My sisters' voices swelled. "Mom!"

"Oh, cut it out," she responded, as if she'd been slighted.

Lia was glaring at her.

"All right. Get in the house," she said, using her body to push us back through the door.

"What about my project?" Sofia asked. My father had promised to drive Sofia to school so her trifold poster wouldn't get wrecked on the bus.

"Oh, don't you worry. He's taking you."

She herded us into the house and marched back toward my father. I watched her yank at his arms until he slid onto the driveway. She wasn't even watching for his head. He woke up chuckling, reaching for the hem of my mother's nightgown with a pinkie finger. "Why, hello, there."

My mother kicked him away. "Not today, Vin." She ran into the house, came back with bottled water in one hand and a couple of salted crackers in the other. "Eat them."

My father thrashed. "Get that out of here."

"Eat the crackers!"

She jabbed one against his lips.

He wriggled, got up on his knees. "Cut it out, would you?"

"Why don't you care?" Her voice was breaking. "Why don't you care about this family?" She was only saying this to him now, when he wouldn't remember.

She uncapped the water and it sloshed over the rim, running down her arms and hands. He snatched the bottle, crushed the crackers in his fist. He pulled himself up and took a few steps, wobbled, and collapsed back on the ground. His shirt was sprinkled with morning dew. One of his shoes had slipped off.

"Get up." She kicked him, her shadow moving across his body. She kicked him again.

"Get." Kick. "Up." Kick. "You have to drive Sofia to school."

He waved his fingers in the air, eyes closed. "Crazy, crazy, crazy, you are fucking crazy," he sang.

I called his name. He opened an eye, quick. I thought maybe he was embarrassed, realizing I was watching. He pointed at me with a crooked finger. "Why don't you drive her?"

"I don't drive," I said.

"Well, you should. You should drive."

"She doesn't drive, Vin. She's fifteen."

He swayed onto his back and spread his arms out, staring up at the pearl-gray sky. "Crazy, crazy. Everyone in this house," he sang, "is mother . . . fucking crazy."

My mind began turning to thoughts of escape. I already spent most of my time alone. I willed time to pass faster. I couldn't wait to leave Topsfield, to start over, to have another chance at making friends, to become someone new. I'd be the first in my family to go to college, and I was impatient to construct this distinction between us, to prove I was nothing like my mother, or even my father, whom I could no longer regard with the same level of pride. He'd appeared threatening to me that day in the driveway—the scar on his cheek standing out newly as a symbol of recklessness and risk. It had changed over the years, becoming redder and darker, impossible to ignore.

24

The house was bound in threatening silence. All of us braced for what was to come. We tried to focus on our homework, keeping our doors cracked open as we waited for our mother to unleash her fury.

When the yelling started, I was sitting on the toilet with the lights off. I peed slowly, at a trickle, so I could make out their words. I didn't flush.

Down the dark hallway to my parents' room, Sofia had already crept outside their door. Lia sat against the hall bookcase with her eyes flicked to the ceiling. I joined her on the floor as we listened to their shouts.

"I don't hold it against *you*, Dee—the way you sulk and moan, eating pills like candy. I don't say anything about the way you behave."

"Don't hold it against me? You don't even *think* about me. You don't want to be *around* me." A drawer slammed.

Lia bumped me with her knee. "I feel like we shouldn't be listening."

I moved to get up.

"You don't have to be anywhere," he said cruelly, mocking.

"You can go or do whatever you want every day of the damn week!"

"I'm done saying anything to you," she said. "Go make a fool of yourself."

"I'm not listening to this. It's comical."

"Drink till you're falling asleep in driveways. Terrify your kids."

We responded with the click of a bedroom door. Sitting in Sofia's room, we listened to their voices fade. There was a moment when I thought about helping my mother, jumping in to defend her. I let it pass. That would have meant turning away from my father, and I couldn't bring myself to acknowledge his failings completely.

That next night, a Saturday, my father insisted we drive to Woburn to get the Bickford's Baby Apple—a baked apple pancake smothered in butter and vanilla ice cream. It was a desperate attempt to smooth things over. My sisters and I had never been there ourselves, but our parents had been talking about it for years.

"Oh, let's go. Let's go," my mother said, falling into the trap. She wrapped her fingers around my father's wrist. "We used to go there as teens after a night of drinking," she told us. And just like that, my sisters and I were knee to knee in the backseat of our mother's car, drifting off to the quiet buzz of the highway, on our way to a giant pancake.

It was a long drive. In half sleep, I could hear my father

messing restlessly with the radio stations, switching from Motown to rock and back to Motown. The car swerved to the left and my right leg pressed on an invisible brake pedal.

"Vin, watch the road."

With my eyes closed, I crossed my fingers and slipped them beneath my thigh. *Nothing bad. Nothing bad.*

It was eleven at night when we slid into a booth of the twenty-four-hour diner. Sweat on the backs of our thighs stuck to the fake leather. I sat with Lia and my mother on one side. Sofia sat on the other with my father. He was leaning over the marbled green tabletop with his fork and knife in either fist, trying to make us laugh. Jim Croce played above us. My father leaned back, released his silverware, and hummed to the song. *Isn't that the way they say it goes? Well, let's forget all that.*

My sisters sat expressionless in their matching Cape Cod sweatshirts, hair pulled back in untidy buns. Our reflections glowed in the window. We looked exactly alike. This would be one of the last times we went out, all of us together—aged fifteen, fourteen, and twelve.

My mother snapped gum as she pointed to the tables with her chin. "We sat in that corner over there with Susan and Tony," she said. "After one of the dances. Remember, hon?"

My father smiled guiltily. "Maybe?"

"Don't take it personally, Diana," I said. "He never remembers anything."

"What's it going to be like when we're eighty?" she asked him. "Will you even remember our first date?"

He covered his face with his hands, betraying himself.

"You're not serious," she said, mad but giggling, spitting a little. She moved to touch his hand and he slipped away, almost instinctively.

"I don't really get why we came here," Sofia said sleepily.

"What, you guys are too old to hang with your parents?" My father piled pink sugar packets onto his fork and catapulted them across the table. His fist came down too hard, and the fork struck my mother's ceramic mug. Coffee splattered on the table.

"Oopsies," my father said. "Pass me a napkin, Soph?"

Sofia groaned, reaching across the table.

"When I used to eat supper at your mother's," my father said, swiping the mess with wide, lazy strokes, "before we were married, there would be this rag in the middle of the table. If you needed to wipe your hands or your mouth you'd have to say, 'Can you pass the rag?' and someone would pass it around the circle and you'd have to use the same dirty, filthy napkin as everyone else."

"What!" My sisters and I woke up at this tale, slamming the table.

My mother let out a syrupy laugh. "It wasn't dirty, filthy. It wasn't that bad."

"Oh, it was so gross." My father scrunched his nose.

"It really was," my mother said, confessing now. She hid her face with her hands, pulled them down, then popped them back up. "I don't know why we did that. Even when my mother was alive," she said, laughing to herself, "we couldn't afford napkins. What do you want me to say?"

"Did *you* use it?" I asked my father.

"I had to!" He put his hands up in defense. "There was nothing else!"

"That's revolting," Lia said. "Seriously, why would you do that?"

My father straightened in his seat, reaching out to smooth the paper napkin in front of him. "Because your mother is what they call 'white trash.'"

"Don't say that, Vin. They'll think it's true."

"It *is* true," he said, breaking into a grin.

"How can that be true when we're from the same place?"

"You're from the icky part of town."

We laughed again.

"You know something else about your mother."

"Stop it, Vin. What are you going to say?"

He kept smiling. "It's bad."

"You're an idiot," she said, kind of laughing.

He pinched his thumb and pointer finger together. "She has an itsy-bitsy teeny-weeny drop of French in her."

"No sir!" She yelped, like my sisters and I even cared. "He's lying."

My father laughed, nodding at us. "Her great-grandmother's maiden name is Beaumont. On the father's side."

"So what?" she said. "That doesn't mean anything."

"My wife is Italian, French, and psychotic," he said, and I knew he was flirting with her, in his own strange way. It was working. She was getting annoyed, but still smiling.

"Did I say 'psychotic'? I meant beautiful." He reached out to touch her hand, tapping the tops of her fingers. "You're beautiful, Dee."

"Keep it up, Vin. First thing you'll see on your desk tomorrow is divorce papers."

"I'm living with Dad!" Lia called out.

"Oh, yeah?" my mother said. "Not in this house. The wife gets everything." She smirked. "Everything."

"Dad's the one who pays for it," I said.

"Yeah, it's not yours," Lia said.

My mother scowled, but recovered quickly. "My name is on everything," she said. "In case someone tries to sue. Tell them, Vin."

My father leaned back in his seat, not seeing the fun in the conversation. "Why are we talking about this?"

"They're the ones saying stuff," my mother said. "Yell at your daughters."

"Whatever," Lia added. "Dad will just buy a bigger and better house and you'll be stuck alone with the guinea pig."

My mother lifted an eyebrow, beaten, as though to say she agreed.

25

That December, we drove out to a holiday party in the sticks of New Hampshire. It was the first time our father had taken us to a work event. After midnight, my sisters and I sat alone at a corner table, strangers to this house and these people. Were his insides sloshing with golden whiskey as he staggered around, laughing exaggeratedly, putting his arm around people?

I knew he'd had a life outside of the family, relationships with people he worked with, an existence we were purposely kept from. Until that night, it had been an abstraction. It made me uneasy now to see the faces of people who knew my father but not my mother, my sisters, or me. People he bantered with, who pulled him into drunken headlocks and laughed at his jokes.

We had never been to this mansion in the woods, or met the host, William Doherty, though we'd been hearing about him for years. We knew our mother couldn't stand him, that she resented our father for indulging him.

At the table, Sofia dismantled her tiramisu, leaving trails of chocolate on the lacy tablecloth as she raked the fabric with her fork. Across from her, Lia chewed gum, snapping it loudly every few minutes. She and I plucked pine needles from the elaborate centerpiece, our reflections warping in the red and green ornaments.

I took in the room of guests, blurred masses of silver and gold, suits of black. Velvet bows of crimson looped around every chair. It was a meld of color, like an impressionist painting.

Since the dinner, an elaborate course of several kinds of fish—lobster, branzino, and baked stuffed sole—our father hadn't come back to our table even once. He hadn't asked Sofia to dance on his feet, the way he sometimes did, or juggled the ornaments so we could fake laugh. At moments, I was sure he didn't remember we were there.

I tossed a pinch of needles on the white tabletop, rolled pine-sap between my thumb and forefinger until it became a tight, gray ball.

My parents started walking toward us, my father swaying to Sinatra's "White Christmas" as he crossed the room. My mother's wine-colored lipstick stood out against her winter complexion. She was wearing the dress she thought best concealed her body; black and lightly sparkled, loose around the waist. She seemed genuinely happy to have my father touching her, hanging on her, whispering gibberish in her ear.

When the desserts were going around, I'd noticed a dark brown spot above her lip. "What's on your face?" I said, reaching out and smudging the mark with my thumb. She pushed me away, frowning, but I had already wiped most of the faux beauty mark from her skin.

Clamoring again for her shoulders, my father swayed. His eyes were like slits.

"Watch it, Vin," she said, swaying herself. Most of her makeup had melted now. She looked like a sad clown. "I'm going to fall over," she said to him.

His eyes were wide, shining like the Christmas lights. In the middle of his forehead pulsed a single vein. It seemed he was losing control of his face, expressions changing from one second to the next.

"Can we go now?" Lia asked. She inched away from my father as he got closer. "Ew, you stink."

"Ooh, what's this?" My father gasped in mock surprise, lowered himself toward her paper plate. "For me?" He stared in drunken wonder at an Italian rainbow cookie, shoved it into his mouth. Then he choked, spurts of red and green erupting from his lips. His cheeks were blood-flushed, his scar showing up angrier. I was mortified, knowing this thing about my father, his drinking, was out in the open for everyone to witness.

When he caught a breath he roared, pounded his fists against his chest like a gorilla. People were looking. When he realized he was the only one laughing, he stopped.

"Doesn't this bother you?" Lia said to my mother, disgusted.

My mother's anger was turning onto us. I could see it in her eyes. "What do you want me to do?" she spat.

We stretched our patience for a few more minutes. But we were begging her to go again as soon as William appeared with a shot glass and a bottle of bourbon. "How about washing that cookie down with some of this?"

"Well, what do we have here?" My father palmed the bottle, inspecting the label.

"Isn't he drunk enough?" I asked my mother.

"Just get your things ready," she whisper-hissed. "We'll leave in a minute." She sifted through the pile of winter coats on the chair beside me.

"Uh-oh," my father said. "She's bringing out the coat." He forgot it was a joke between him and my sisters. My mother didn't know we made fun of her dress-up coat, pea green. "Anna," he said. "The ugly coat."

My mother studied the coat in her arms, confused, and then narrowed her eyes at me.

William put a hand on my mother's shoulder. "Dee, we have plenty of room upstairs. Pillows and blankets for the kids. Don't make him drive all the way home."

"Oh, I'm fine," our father said, waving his hand dismissively and pulling his keys from his pocket. He gave them a reassuring jingle.

I had to concentrate to not slip on ice. Gripping the iron railing out the front door with white-knuckled fists, I made my way down to the walkway. My mother went slowly behind me, two feet on each step, like a child. My father was yards ahead, pretending to surf down the driveway as he headed toward her car.

"Why don't we just stay?" I asked her. "Mr. Doherty said they have room."

"I don't want to wake up here," my mother said.

"None of us do. But isn't that better than this?" I asked, gesturing toward my father.

"What am I supposed to wear to sleep? I'm not going to fit in that woman's clothes." She was referring to William's tiny wife.

At the car, my sisters snapped the handles of the locked doors. My father slipped and slid on a patch of ice, catching himself just in time, laughing.

"Mom, look at him. He's not okay."

"No shit, he's not okay. I've been telling him he's not okay. He has to keep up with his friends even though they're twice his size. I married a moron."

"That's not the point. You can't let him do this."

She spun around. "Say it to *him*, Anna. Why should I listen to this?"

"Because Dad's drunk." I couldn't believe I had to explain this to her. "You're the mother."

She got close, almost knocking me over. She was about to say something but decided to keep it to herself. I grasped the railing with two hands, descended the stairs and out of the porch light, into the deep cold.

The roads were motionless, dark and wet with slush. The pavement shone like glass. In the beam of headlights, the legs of the forest glowed on either side of us. With one hand on the wheel, my father rummaged through the center console and pulled out one of my mother's loose CDs.

"Let's see what we have here," he said, jamming it into the drive.

My mother shook her head, irritated.

Elton John came on and my father cheered, tapping his fingers on the wheel like a pretend pianist. He rolled down the windows. "To keep from falling asleep," he said. Ice-wind slithered down my dress, but the heat was cranked up and my eyes watered from the blasts of hot and cold air.

Beside me, Lia rested with her head straight back, lips parted, eyes closed. Her head wobbled from the bumps on the road, and I wondered how she could sleep like that. On my other side, Sofia was peeling the wrappers from her reindeer-shaped chocolates, taking a bite of each, testing them to see if they tasted the same.

My father swerved over the yellow lines, singing about highways and sheets of linen. My stomach tumbled each time he swooped too close to the snow that was banked in rough mounds, too close to the trees. They were skeletal, branches stretching.

I twisted around for a look out the back window, squinting at the peak of the hill, waiting for the blue lights. I was sure this would be the night my father was caught, that someone would stop him. In that moment, I wanted it to happen. I wanted relief.

"You're getting it all over you," I said to Sofia, her lap filled with foil and naked chocolates, each baring her teeth marks. I counted the chocolates to concentrate on something else.

"Who cares. This dress is ugly anyway," she said, pulling at her three-quarter-length sleeves. She chewed on the tinfoil because she liked the way it felt on her teeth.

Lia was slumped to the side now, her head pressed against the window. A warm cloud dilated where her breath hit the glass.

As my father sang, my mother gave him a long, hard look, scooted closer to the window.

I felt a nudge on my arm.

"Guess which hand," Sofia said, holding two fists in front of me.

"Huh?"

"Which hand?"

I must have looked confused.

"Guess and I'll give you one," she said. "Come on, just pick. Left or right."

"That one—"

Air caught in my throat as we careened across the road and into the woods, where the soil and rocks gave way and we slid like a flume ride into a ditch. I lunged forward, slamming my head against the front seat, my stomach dropping as we plunged. It happened fast—branches snapping, debris and rocks pelting the windshield. There was screaming. Objects flew around inside the car—bottle caps, loose pens, and papers. I had to use my hands to steady my head as it jerked to either shoulder. There were grunts and squeals from my sisters, gasping, confused breaths. We creaked to a stop. The car let out its last sigh.

An eerie silence except for the crunching of the forest, branches clicking away beneath the weight of snow. The car was slanting, my sisters and me piled to the right, crushing Lia. I tried to talk. My mouth was pooling with blood.

Sofia pulled herself up, holding on to her arm, limp. We

would find out later that she had fractured her wrist, broken a finger. There was blood running from her mouth down her chin and she was frowning, her tongue probing her gums, the space where a tooth had been.

I slipped two fingers inside my own mouth, pinched my tongue to stop the pain. I must have bit it when the car reeled forward.

When my father spoke, his voice was clogged. He tried again, face contorting in agony as he attempted to look over his shoulder. "Girls?"

"We're okay," Lia said. Her head glimmered red, shiny streams of the color trickling down the side. She wavered a little, dizzy. I could hear the blood beat in my ears, feel the panic searing in my gut. My mother hadn't spoken.

"Dee?" He flung out his right arm, flailed, tried to grab her. His body was contorted, wedged between the steering wheel and the door.

My mother's neck was bent in an unnatural position, as if she were about to rest it on her shoulder, but decided not to. She whimpered like a small animal. The sound made me want to cry but I couldn't. My father's two fingers ran softly across her hand.

I tried to stretch forward but my seat belt jerked me back, digging into my stomach.

My mother gripped the armrest with both hands. "I can't move my neck," she said.

My father wriggled free. "It'll be okay, Dee." His voice sounded young.

"There was an animal," he added.

"An animal?" my mother asked through uneven breaths.

"No one saw it?" My father looked at us through the rearview mirror. "You didn't see it, Dee? Right in the middle of the road."

I was so sad for him in that moment. I leaned back in my seat, feeling my heart, desperate for it to calm down. Beside me, Lia let out sharp breaths, holding her head. She was never one to complain, always strong.

Sirens howled in the distance. At the top of the ditch, strangers stood on the road, peering down at us. My father was in trouble, and his silence, the way he kept swallowing, told me he didn't have a plan. He wasn't getting out of it.

"Tell them, Vin," my mother said quietly. "There was an animal."

My right arm was starting to sting. Sofia was latched on to me, her nails digging into the crook of my elbow. Later, at the Portsmouth Regional Hospital, I would notice the crescent-shaped marks on my arm.

Our father climbed out, pulled us from the backseat. He didn't dare to move my mother. My sisters and I stood groggy and mute in the cold, looking with disbelief at our mother's car. The front was smashed, crinkled, the open hood squeezed into a terrible grimace. There were branches stuck in odd places. The license plate hung by a single screw.

The impossible thought that we hadn't actually survived occurred to me. I stomped a foot on the ground to make sure this was all real, I was really here.

A pair of men slid down the snow and the dirt to see if we were okay. A strange woman put her arms around me. More minutes passed and an ambulance finally pulled up. When the EMTs hauled my mother onto a stretcher, she pressed her thighs together. She'd forgotten her underwear that morning. That's what she whispered to me as she tugged on my arm, frantic with fear, imploring me to come with her into the ambulance.

Our parents were pulled off in different directions and we were led to a police cruiser. A young, pasty officer sat up front. He shook a box of orange Tic Tacs in front of us, trying to offer comfort. As if we were children.

I won't forget the sight of my father's silhouette in headlights, his hands in cuffs, head slumped in humiliation. The twinkle of shattered glass on pavement. And my mother, yards ahead, twitching and moaning, held fixed by the straps, as if she were about to be electrocuted.

More drivers stood by their cars at the side of the road. They'd pulled over not to see if we were okay, but to see what would happen to my father, the one responsible. He had bloodshot eyes—red from alcohol, or tears.

He'd made a scene, laughing when the officers commanded him to take the breathalyzer, to recite the alphabet. I recalled him stumbling—trying and failing to say it backward. The officers shook their heads, sickened by him, sorry for us.

Jesus, man. With your kids in the car.

I remember the ambulance, dust and exhaust and debris cutting glares into bright lights.

I've asked myself many times how we got there, to that moment, on that road in the dead of night. Standing there, a sense of what it was that I was watching—what my sisters and I had been watching for all these months, years—snapped into place. My father was no longer a solid, unimpeachable mass of responsibility and authority, whose direction I followed, whose intimacy I sought, whose admiration I longed for. In that moment, every word my mother had used against him seemed to ring with truth. I didn't blame him. Still. After everything. I couldn't blame him.

The situation seemed ridiculous to me. The sudden desire to laugh arose, then vanished, replaced by a panicky urge to run. To flee from the accumulating betrayals, the lies and secrets and silence and mess, everything that had mounted inside that vast, airless house, until the five of us had become strangers to one another. I knew, already, looking one last time at my mother and father being pulled away, that we were a family lost.

26

I rinsed my mouth with tap water until the bleeding stopped. Crimson bits settled in the cracks of my teeth. At the hospital, I stood by Lia as the nurse sewed five stitches into her forehead. And when Sofia had her wrist cast, I held the other hand. We wanted tea afterward, but only had a crumpled dollar. We took turns trying to iron it with our palms. We split the tea while we sat in the waiting room, Sofia holding ice to her mouth. The metallic bite in mine lingered.

"I look like a monster," she said, looking at her reflection on her cell phone, tonguing the hole where her tooth had been. Her eyes were tearing.

"They'll fix it, Soph." I gave her shoulder a squeeze.

"Will they fix it so you won't be able to tell?"

"Of course. Don't you remember the Ignagni boys from Everett? One of them threw a pool table ball at the other's face. Chipped his tooth right here." I pointed to my left front tooth. "You'd never know today."

A couple of hours later, around three in the morning, we heard a commotion down the hall. All of a sudden Trisha was there, bursting through the double doors in mismatched pajamas. It was unexpected and took me several beats to recognize her. "Oh, girls!" Her shouting made us self-conscious. "Are you okay?" What a strange sight, surreal. I could understand my father's desperation. There was no one else he could have called; he would never let his mother or brothers see him in this state.

"They won't let us see Mom," I said, meeting her halfway so she wouldn't get too close to my sisters.

Trisha knelt to the ground, placing her fingertips on their knees. "You need to be strong girls while the doctors fix her up," she said, talking to us like we were babies. She pulled all three of us into her at once. "Come with me," she said, leading us to the exit. "We have to get your father."

I pulled from her grasp. "Can we stay here with Mom?"

Trisha seemed genuinely sorry. "I'm afraid your father needs you. They're more likely to let him out if they see you girls. If they see you waiting for him."

She wasn't wrong. The officer said as much when my father eventually stumbled into the station's waiting room, making some smart-ass comment I couldn't fully hear.

"Keep it up, man. If it weren't for these girls you'd be spending the night here."

I studied Trisha on the ride home. Her skin smelled of lavender, nails clean and bare, no jewelry except for the gold chain around her neck. Tiny bumps around her mouth and chin were her only imperfections. My bailed-out father was silent in the passenger seat. Trisha didn't ask him any questions, didn't probe or overstep, the way I'd expected her to. I knew she wouldn't be coming around anymore after this.

She dropped us off at the house around six in the morning. It occurred to me that we'd never been here without our mother. Her spot in the living room was still, waiting, and I became conscious of the unusual quiet—only the whistle of the heater, the creak of the windows.

My father rummaged through every drawer and cabinet in the kitchen, piling random foods onto the table—cheeses, nuts, and graham crackers. We weren't hungry. It felt wrong to be eating. The table was cluttered with tape and bows and rolls of wrapping paper—the way our mother had left it. In the living room, Christmas lights scattered colors across the floor. I tried to retrieve yesterday's feelings—the comfort of wrapping presents with my mother and sisters, bickering over the last red bow. Could we just go back there? How did everything change so quickly?

Bits of gravel clicked across my molars. There was a scratching sensation when I rotated my eyes.

Across from me, Sofia was sniffling and fingering a run in her tights. Lia tore at paper napkins, rolling them into snakes, the way my mother did. Her eyes were shiny with tears she refused to let fall. We were powerless, trapped in impatient exhaustion.

We wanted to know what had happened to our mother, wanted to find her, make sure she was okay. We didn't know whom to ask.

I needed to change out of my dress. Sequins dug in at the sleeves and neckline, forming a raised, pink rash. When I asked if we should go upstairs to change, my sisters shook their heads. I stayed at the table because I didn't want to go up there alone. I didn't want to do anything alone.

My father hadn't said a word. There were bruises on his hands and forearms, bloodied nicks on his knuckles. His eyes were purpled from the airbag. I studied him at the end of the table, his head buried in his hands. His rumpled hair glimmered beneath the light, shining with specks of something—I couldn't tell what. My jaw clamped when I made the connection. It wasn't bits of pebble planted in the grooves of my teeth. It was tiny shards of glass. What if I'd swallowed a piece? Would the remains prick my intestines? I didn't ask my father, didn't want to trouble him with any questions.

He grunted and the three of us swiveled to face him.

"I'm going to see your mother," he said. "You girls get some rest."

"What?" Lia and Sofia said at the same time.

He stood up, slacks wrinkled, dress shirt untucked. A stain on his collar. "She's all alone," he muttered, disoriented. Or drunk. It was hard to tell. "And I have to deal with the car."

"Maybe you shouldn't drive," I said, anxious. Why couldn't he make one right decision?

"Yeah, okay. I'll call a taxi."

"Can't we come?" Sofia asked.

"I'll get you later," he said.

"Why can't we come?"

The question halted him, stiffened his back. "I'm sorry, girls." His voice was high and unfamiliar, eyes glazed. "I messed up. I'm so sorry." He no longer resembled our father but a person on the verge of splitting open. Letting his upper half collapse on the counter, he shook his head at some invisible thing in front of him. He started to cry, briefly. Then he sniffed hard, pulled himself upright. "I'll call you in bit." He cleared his throat. "It's going to be okay. Get some rest."

I knew I wouldn't sleep. Simmering in me was a feeling I was afraid to identify—a quiet thrill that my sisters and I were alone, free of our parents.

My body hummed with anxiety, intensified by every move my sisters made, like when they went to the sink for water or turned on the icemaker, when Sofia bopped rolls of wrapping paper on the table. Why couldn't everyone be still? Just for a few moments?

I'd heard of people blacking out in accidents, remembering only parts of the experience. That wasn't the case for me. Everything replayed in my head, over and over. Flashes of light and screaming and blood. I kept thumbing my eyelids, trying to push the images out.

"What if she's really hurt," I said.

"She's fine," Lia said.

"You don't know that, though. I wish we'd asked how bad it was. Why didn't we ask the doctors at the hospital?"

Neither of them responded. Lia typed on her cell phone with her thumbs.

"Who're you texting at six in the morning?" I asked. I couldn't look away from the bandage on her forehead.

"My friends."

"You can't tell anyone what happened, Lia. Not a single person."

"You can't tell me what to do."

"They'll never look at Dad the same. Your friends won't be allowed over here."

She scoffed.

"It's personal, Lia. Why do your friends need to know every little thing about your life?"

"Screw you, Anna. You don't know what I'm feeling. What's going on in my head." She tossed her phone on the table, got up. "I need some real food."

"There's nothing in this house," said Sofia, her head in her hands. The yelling—the way Lia and I treated each other—was hurting Sofia. I should have stopped, but I was opening my mouth to yell more.

Sofia banged the table, told me no with her eyes.

Across the room, Lia poked around inside the cabinets. "Where there's a will, there's a way!" She raised a box of Cheerios in the air in triumph.

"How old are those?" Sofia asked.

Lia checked the box, paused, then poured the cereal into a bowl. "It's going to be weird when she's back," she said.

"Weird, how?" asked Sofia.

"I don't know." She pulled milk from the fridge. "Like, how do you live with the knowledge that your husband almost killed you?"

"Can you not be so vulgar?" I said.

"Well, it's true. They've been killing each other for years."

Maybe it was true. I didn't know why we had to talk about it. Maybe it was better if we kept our thoughts to ourselves.

Lia yelped and jumped back from the counter. Her hands clapped over her mouth. "Oh my God. I'm going to throw up."

"What is it?" I asked.

"There're fucking ants in the cereal."

Sofia and I hurried over. The tiny bodies squirmed in the milk, climbing onto the Cheerios as if they were lifeboats.

27

That evening, I woke disoriented with my face pressed against a blanket. Damp fibers clung to my cheek. A pressure on my chest told me something terrible had happened. Then I remembered.

My sisters were asleep beside me on Lia's bed, both of them inched toward the top, their knees pulled up to their chins. We'd been watching reruns of some reality show, agreeing without discussion that we would stay close until our father came home.

I made my way to my parents' room, flipped the switch, and my mother's bureau lit into view. There was a burning in my eyes as I played with the gold earrings in the porcelain tray, as I studied the photos taped to the mirror. There was one of each of us, Lia, Sofia, and me, each snipped into crooked hearts, another with us girls—my mother kneeling on cobblestones on Disney's Main Street, U.S.A., her arms around our tiny waists. We wore plastic mouse ears pinned with pink bows, my mother clad in her white shorts and tennis shoes and the fuchsia shirt with the golden grommets. It was the only time we went to Disney, and we were too young to remember it. I didn't know how long the photo had been there. When was the last time I'd been in her room? My chest was cramping. I felt sick. I pulled open a dresser drawer for distraction. In it I found tiny bonnets and a pair of moccasins, relics from our past, little treasures. I imagined my mother's fingers tying the strings around our baby chins.

I wanted to sit beside her, watch over her. Dropping my elbows on the bureau, I weighed my head in my hands, willing myself not to cry. I knew that once I started, I wouldn't be able to stop.

There was a rustling in the bed.

"Jesus! You scared me."

My father sat up, unable to open his eyes all the way. "What are you doing?"

I was shocked to find my mother lying flat beside him, strapped in a neck brace, fast asleep. "When did you come home?" I made my way to her side.

"She's on a heavy dose of painkillers," he said.

The clock radio glowed on the nightstand—6:45 p.m.

"We got back a few hours ago. You girls were out cold."

I stopped myself, not wanting to get too close. I wrapped my fingers around the bedpost, watching her sleep. That's when I noticed the cane propped against the nightstand.

"Is that forever?" I asked my father.

"We don't know yet."

I went back to bed and woke many hours later. In my room, I charted the cracks on the ceiling as I followed the sounds below me in the kitchen—the running faucet and cabinets thudding, someone smacking onto the couch. I knew from his throat-clearing that it was my father.

Soon the *Charlie Brown* theme song resounded throughout the house, a timely familiarity. My mother watched it every Christmas, said it reminded her of her own mother.

My phone started vibrating under the covers. The house was calling. "Hello?"

"Are you awake?"

My mother.

"Can you make me some mac and cheese?" she asked.

"Why don't you have Dad make it?"

"Because. Come hang out with me."

When I got downstairs, my father was already asleep. I left the television on, hoping it would keep him settled. I couldn't imagine what was going through his mind, couldn't help but feel sorry for him.

Then, sitting beside my mother, I listened to the scrape of silver against metal as she ate macaroni straight from the pot, propped up in her neck brace. The sound put my teeth on edge. "You want some?" Her inner thighs were scorched pink from keeping the pot in her lap. She dug out the fork, tried handing it over to me.

"I'm okay."

"Have some." She crammed her mouth with another bite. "Use my dish."

"Does it hurt?" I asked, pointing to the brace.

"Those painkillers work miracles. But I can't stop eating."

"You think it's the pills?"

"I've heard they can do that." She gestured to her pot. "Take some."

I took the fork from her, scooped up some macaroni.

"We probably should have stayed last night," she said. "Doherty's place."

"Probably," I said, stretching the word out.

"He's going to be in a lot of trouble. Your father."

"Like, he's going to go to jail?"

"I don't know about that, but he'll lose his license. You girls will be driving us around." She studied the pot as if there were nothing left to be said.

"How long do you have to wear that?" I asked.

"A month, I think?" She picked a noodle out with her fingers, put it on her tongue. She chewed methodically, too slow for such a small bite. Then her cheeks ballooned. Out of nowhere, she started to hysterically cry. I put down the fork, alarmed.

"Does it hurt?" I asked.

"He was going to leave me, Anna. The woman who does the checks? The one who picked you up from the hospital?"

I nodded, watching her tears fall freely. They pooled at the edge of the neck brace. I'd never seen somebody sob like that, silently, as if she were using all of her might not to breathe in, as if to take in air would be to realize her sadness anew, to usher in a new wave of pain.

"Stop," I said, chasing her tears with that same word, over and over. I wanted to put my hand on her arm, but couldn't make myself do it. "You don't know that he did anything," I said stupidly.

"Don't protect him, Anna. You're always protecting him. It wasn't just me he was leaving," she said. "He was going to leave the three of you too. All of us."

"I don't think he would have done that." I swallowed and tensed my muscles, braced for her next biting attack. It didn't come. At least, not in the way I expected.

"Because he can do no wrong in your eyes."

It was the way she said it—with such conviction—that made me lose my temper. I was so tired of being blamed. "That's not true. I know he messed up. I know he's not perfect. But he apologizes. You never apologize—" I could feel myself boiling over, losing control of my words.

"What the hell do you want me to apologize for?"

"I asked you if we could stay! I was scared and I didn't want to get in the car with him and you made us. You insisted! Even though you knew he couldn't drive."

"Oh, so it's my fault?"

"It's both of you!" I was finally crying, though I didn't want to be. I couldn't control it.

"Go to your room if you're going to talk to me like this!"

"It's the truth—"

"So, it's my fault we crashed into a ditch? It's my fault your sister has to get fake teeth?"

"You weren't looking out for us. No other mother would have done what you did."

"Get out of my face, if you're going to be talking to me like this." She was breathing fast and hard. "Comparing me to other mothers! Who do you know who has such a great mother?"

"Any of them are better than you," I screamed, not caring if I woke my father or sisters.

She lunged like she might hit me, then gasped and reached for her neck.

Down the hall, a door creaked open.

"I can say the same about you, Anna. You think I'd be where I am today if it weren't for the three of you? All your clinging and bitching. Always taking your father's side. Always 'feeling bad' for your father," she said, talking in a whining baby voice, imitating me.

"I do feel sorry for him. Because he has to deal with *you*." I was done. They'd both failed, and I'd almost gotten killed be- cause of it. I wiped my face and then left her, crying in her food.

That night, in a dream, my mouth filled with sludge—a yellow- white substance that continued to sprout despite how quickly I dug and emptied it in the toilet. When I woke, my tongue was strained, jaw heavy and tense. I was sick with regret.

We never addressed what happened that night. In the morn- ing, she behaved as though everything were normal. But I couldn't take back my words, and I could never again be alone with her in a room, not without thinking about the terrible things we'd said to each other.

This made things difficult, as my mother's injuries made her reliant on us. To wash, she sat on a fold-up chair in the shower, the splatter of water on plastic resounding throughout the house. I passed the open door one morning, spotting her hazed figure through the blue-green glass of the shower door. I helped her bathe, standing in the shower stream as I detangled her hair with my fingers. So many strands fell out, stretching for the drain like tentacles.

When the neck brace was finally removed, she was still in pain. An aching in the joints and bends of her body. That's when the crying started. Despairing moans in the middle of the night. It angered me to hear her weeping, using the pills to cope and numb herself, long after she needed them for the pain. None of us bothered to ask what it was she was trying to forget.

My sisters and I started staying across the street at Vera's, leaving our father to take care of her. We lay on Vera's rug with pillows and blankets, listening to Kiss 108 while we plucked our brows or painted our nails. She belonged to all of us now. "It'll be okay," she'd say, taking turns shrouding us in her arms. It was the only good thing to come out of that mess—my reawakened friendship with Vera. That, and my father's sobriety.

All the while, my mother paced the house with an immovable sadness, grasping walls and countertops for support, refusing to use her cane. Helpless, desperate, she pulled at the skin of her face and neck. Inflamed patches bloomed like flowers on her freckled chest.

I was ten again, the age I was when we left Everett, watching my mother vanish before me. The living room now belonged to her, mildewed and cluttered, several degrees warmer than the rest of the house. It was a nest for crusty yogurt cups and depleted water bottles, beaten magazines slopped in a pile. Everything was strategically placed to limit her movements. Objects multiplied until the room itself shrunk and faded, resembling a woodman's cottage. She enjoyed being close to the television with the local news on mute while she doodled in her magazines, said the electric hum felt good in her head.

There were days it seemed she was getting better, like the afternoon I found her outside on the swinging bench, filling a bowl of nuts for the chipmunks, clicking her tongue when they scurried over. Or a few months later, when she met a flock of wild turkeys at the rock wall and fed them slices of wheat bread. These moments were fleeting. It came down to her flesh fighting against her, the painkillers prescribed by her doctors, year after year. The thing she wanted most, to be taken care of, became the thing she most resented.

I often thought about that rainy morning in Everett, sitting on the stained blue sofa with salami-and-cheese roll-ups. I wished I could return to that moment. I wished I could protest when my father announced the move. But we were only capable of silence then. If we'd stayed in that house, we could have spent more time together, the five of us. Could have had extra money for summer vacations in Italy, walking our feet sore through Sicily, like my mother dreamed. We could have gone on the second trip to Florida that never happened, even though we spent weeks fantasizing about the deep end of the pool, our parents clinking daiquiris under the shade of a palm tree. Our mother could have been happy in Everett, taking her morning walks downtown, coming back with treats and trinkets from the flea market, fresh pasta and cured meats from the Italian marketplace. My father could have come home to a peaceful house, filled with laughter and warmth. Maybe staying there wouldn't have mattered. Either way, I never told her this. I never said out loud that we should have stayed in that house, never gave her that peace. I should have known to protect her.

28

The summer I left, my last before college, my life was on pause. I no longer sought out small daily pleasures, like sunning in the yard, basking in the cottony rip of grass as I pulled it in clumps. Most of my time was spent alone in my room, questioning if it was right to leave my family behind. At least I could bring a piece of home to New York. Vera was coming with me.

Lia thought it was selfish of me to go to college so far away, on purpose. She told me this the day I accepted my admission. In the weeks leading up to my departure, she barely said a word to me. I left my door ajar, hoping she might stop in. But she avoided my room as if it contained some sort of disease, scampering quickly at the staircase landing and slamming her door. I worried that she might take it out on the rest of the family, on Sofia, but this behavior seemed uniquely reserved for me.

The weather was insufferable that July, and my mother had a hard time breathing in the heat. To keep cool, Sofia and I took her to the air-conditioned shops in the next town over. She fanned herself with pamphlets she picked up at the register, pushed her carriage slowly through the home decor section, pausing at bundles of hand towels and fancy soap dispensers, her cane tucked beneath her arm.

"Oh, that would look great in the guest bathroom, don't you think, Anna?" Her voice would be high, self-conscious, seeking. She wanted to be overheard.

I made efforts to attend to her, but never in public. With enough distance, no one would know I belonged to her. Hangers clinked, giving other mothers in jogging suits away as they glimpsed over aisles to get a look, showing the whites of their eyes. We migrated deeper into the store to avoid the sight, her voice.

Back on the street, we were ashamed of her frantic shuffles, how she held her breath when someone passed, as if it would make her vanish. It didn't seem natural for her to be out of the house. We were sorry for her, but we neither defended nor comforted her, fooling ourselves into thinking that she was oblivious to it all.

I was sick the morning I left, first in the toilet, then in a shopping bag next to my bed. My bare knees dug into floorboards as my insides splattered into plastic. The nervous throwing up would happen again on the train to New York, only then I was alone, my family behind me. None of the passengers said a word when I hunched forward in my seat, heaving a stream of vinegary bile into my scarf. No one looked up. Through the window,

New England trees, rivers, and lawns blurred to golds and greens, rushed into the past.

As I carried the last bag to my father's truck, my sisters were just getting out of bed. I could hear them in the green bathroom—the swish of the plastic curtain, the knocking of pipes as one of them turned on the shower. I shouted goodbye from the bottom of the staircase. They called out from the bathroom, voices sleepy, unable to handle an early morning, an important moment, with sincerity or grace. My father made them come down.

Sofia was already sniffling.

"Jesus, Soph," Lia said. "New York's not even that far."

But we wouldn't be able to see each other without hopping on a five-hour train. We wouldn't be able to get to one another in an emergency.

"It is too," Sofia said, and I was thankful for this response, to be missed. Sofia's hair was a bit snarled, standing up in different directions. She still seemed so small to me, even though she was fifteen.

When we hugged goodbye, we didn't really touch, just pressed our collarbones together. We didn't say any final words. With age, we grew embarrassed to compliment each other, to even say thank you after we opened a gift. To say a word of kindness to a sister. These are virtues taught by the mother.

She was waiting for me in the living room. I was afraid to say goodbye to her. By then, she was practically living on the couch. The burgundy leather had turned dry and cracked beneath her weight, and on the spot that pillowed her head of unwashed hair lived a permanent splotch of oil. Sunlight came through the bay windows of the living room, landing in rectangles on the ashen floorboards, illuminating the stray hairs that clung to her wool socks. On the side table sat a porcelain bowl of plum tomatoes, connected to the vine, which my mother plucked and bit into like apples. Tomato juice trickled down her arms, pooling in the fabric of her nightgown.

"You sure you don't want to come for the ride?" I asked. I didn't feel angry or sad. I didn't expect much. A fear had taken over that something might go wrong, that I might never make it to New York. Maybe I'd miss the train or it'd be canceled. Maybe my mother would ask me not to go.

She'd been proud when I first received my acceptance letters, but only over the schools that were close to home. Once I'd made my choice, the pride faded. Like Lia, she sensed this was the first step to complete separation.

"Did you hear me?" I asked.

When she shifted, there was a crinkling sound and the silver glint of a wrapper jammed between the cushions. An orange vial of pills slipped and rattled from behind her back. My mother draped an arm over the spot as if to hide it and I looked away. On the blackened windowsills, dirt-colored moths lay half dead, twitching in the glint of light.

"Are there spare sheets?" I asked. "For my dorm room?" I wanted to ask something, anything to get her talking.

"In the garage." She stuck a finger inside her coffee cup to fish out a slice of ice cube, her way of saying no. It seemed a bad combination—the acrid taste of coffee and tomato.

When I turned, I saw her bowed head reflected in the glass doors of the fireplace, the heels of her palms pressing against wet eyes.

Outside, the rosebushes looked rotten, and my mother's herb garden lay abandoned beneath the window. The grass was dried and yellowed, overtaken by grubs.

I walked down the path to the garage, searched for the box of extra linens. I found it beside the old dollhouse—half shingled and partially painted, never furnished. When I opened the box, the sheets and pillowcases were moldy. I left them and slowly made my way to the truck, biding my time. I didn't know what I was waiting for, what it was that I wanted. Eventually, I climbed into my father's Chevy. He'd just gotten his license back. It was one of my first times driving with him, but I felt strangely safe. The air was thick with late summer heat. The leather seats scalded my thighs. As we backed down the driveway, I caught a glimpse of my mother by the front window—her paisley nightgown a flash behind the glass.

I believe that long after she's gone, she will be permanently attached to that house. The wooden floors will groan beneath the weight of her steps. She'll live and breathe in the walls.

29

Together on our little couch, in our apartment that's dark and heavy with grief, Vera scrolls to Sofia's name in my phone. She puts the call on speaker.

Sofia asks me to come home, not for our mother or father, but for her and Lia. "We don't have to talk. We can just sit together. Be there together." She isn't asking much of me, and hearing her voice, understanding and gentle, I have no choice but to book the next train.

She tells me they found her in the garage, legs strewn awkwardly. My mother was watching one of her shows when she thought she heard a bird, got up to follow its wings. When she opened the door and peered into the pitch black, there wasn't a thing in sight. But she swore she could hear the creature, its beak clicking at car tires. She moved forward with no one to hold on to her as she took her first step, no one to catch her when she started leaning, to hear her tumble down the stairs. No one to hear the silence afterward, to see the dust rising from the ground when she landed. She lay that way crumpled in the cold, unable to move, waiting.

It was my father who found her, coming home from work some hours later. He almost crashed pulling in when he spotted her at the bottom of the steps, elbows raw, nightgown bunched at her stomach. He was certain she was dead until he saw her head tipping back, looking at him from upside down.

He kept the dispatcher on the phone until the ambulance arrived. I imagined him stroking my mother's hair, telling her it would be okay, covering her right thigh, which was mottled black and blue.

When he heard the siren, he opened the garage doors. My mother moaned as the EMTs strapped her in. My father was about to hop in the ambulance when he spotted the neighbors, hands over mouths, clutching robes and porch railings at twilight.

"She was so out of it," Sofia said, nearing the end of the call. "Me and Lia flushed the pills."

When I arrive at the station, my father is waiting for me. It's silent for the first few minutes in his truck. Hot air blows from his heaters, the warmth intensifying the scent of nuggets and fries. I'm not ready to look back on this Boston cityscape, to be thrust into what I've left behind. It's impossible not to give in to the nostalgia, to immortalize my younger self. It's been three years. I'm afraid to walk through that door.

He asks me about work and about Vera.

"How's New York?" he says, like she's an old friend.

The closer we are to the house, the more distant he becomes, less aware of me. Now my mother is his priority. "She's not doing too good," he announces, like it's news. "I've been away a lot. Traveling for work. And that whole thing in the garage," he says, shaking his head.

I make a sound to say I've heard him.

"She's off the pills, though. Your sisters were a big help. They've been at the house around the clock, making sure she's eating good, drinking water. They flushed it all down the toilet. Every bottle."

"I heard." My brain knows he isn't guilting me, but it still feels that way.

"The fish will be feeling good," he says, laughing. "I've been making her these green smoothie drinks the past couple of weeks. You mix in some citrus and you can't even taste the spinach. I try to get her to turn off the TV before bed, to regulate her hours. With that sleep apnea her body never rests. Then she wakes up in all this joint pain."

I pinch my lips into an expression that's half frown, half pitiful smile. What does he want me to say? I steal a sideward glance at him. He's starting to lose his looks. His once thick hair is thinning at the temples, turning silver to match the edges of his beard. I can't look at him too closely, not without being sad. I long for the days of his woody aftershave and sun-bronzed skin, his brightness, his easy smile.

"If she'd never got on those painkillers, after what happened in New Hampshire . . ." That's how he refers to the accident. *That thing that happened.* "If she just pushed through it . . ." He leans closer to the wheel. "We're going to get her back on track," he says, reassuring himself.

I've heard it all before. And I'm tired. When is he going to learn that he has no control over her? That talking about this won't solve a thing?

Our school photos are still taped to the dashboard—the three of us in lacy collared dresses, frowning at the camera. The paper is crinkled and sun-bleached. I don't forget his nights away, the drinking, his absence. The rational part of me knows that he is more than the sum of his faults. But it's difficult sitting beside him. I think of that night, the one we don't talk about, the one we've set aside with all the things we don't say. It's quiet for a long time. A reserve that is colored with sorrow.

It starts to snow.

He puts on his blinker, switches lanes and speeds up.

I burn when I think of Vera. With my mother on my mind, I almost forgot what happened. "I'm not going to just forget about this," she said as I was leaving. "We'll talk when you're back." And then: "Be good, Anna."

"She wasn't always like this," my father says, cutting my thoughts.

I watch the flakes swirling, whipping the lights.

"She grew up without a mother. That's got to be hard."

I can feel the tears welling, out of frustration, anger, mostly fear. I'm afraid of where the conversation will go. I don't want to talk about her. Only now am I fully hit with the realization that I'm going to see her.

"To tell you the truth, I never knew much about your grandmother. Your mother never talks about her. But. She needed her." His voice comes back into focus. "It wasn't so bad when we were younger, when we were dating, but it hit her when she had you girls."

I pull at my fingers, starting to sweat. He's never talked this much, for so long.

"It's easy to say she should have gotten herself together, but she was young with three small kids. Some people can do it. I don't know. Others need help. Anna, the fact that I did nothing of any significance—seek professional or medical help for her— is the single biggest regret of my life."

I let that hang in the air for a moment. I run my hands over my jeans, straighten in my seat. "What did she used to be like?"

"She was hopeful, confident. She used to commute into Boston by train every day for work, if you can believe it. She worked at that day care center."

Yes. At one time I had known this about my mother. It's hard to imagine her as a young woman on the T, traveling in work clothes, but I try.

"What else?" I ask, softening.

"Specifics?" He laughs. "I don't know. I'm not good at this stuff."

We veer off Route 1, away from the lights and the highway. Naked trees line the edge of the road, bony branches reaching toward the blue-black sky.

"She was pretty, you know. I know you've seen pictures, but she was really beautiful."

"I know."

"Smart. Always has been."

I laugh. "Now you're exaggerating."

"I mean it," he says. "In different ways. She knows people. She can peg anyone who walks through the door. She'll look at them for five minutes and go, 'That person's this and that,' and I'll say, 'How can you know that? You just met them!'"

"She just likes talking shit," I say, laughing a little.

"Maybe. But I can't do that. I can't know a person by the looks of them. Do you know how many people have screwed me over the years? I don't know a person's true colors until it's too late. After your mother has warned me a bunch of times. We fill each other in. What she can't do, I can do, and vice versa.

"Don't be so hard on her," he adds.

I like the sound of his words. *We fill each other in.*

Our town is coming into view. The snow-packed forest replaces the fields and the hills wavering behind them.

30

I was last home during Christmas, before my final semester of college. Sofia had a serious boyfriend who went to snowmen-building contests and drove her to tree farms—who stood with her in the heated, pine-scented store, and who sucked on honey sticks while he lugged the tree into the back of his truck. That's where they were the night I came home for the holiday break. When they arrived at the house, after we said our tongue-tied hellos, the two of them took the mini tree up to Sofia's room. Lia followed them through the door, making an effort not to say anything when she saw me sitting with our mother.

For dinner, we set up in the living room with the television going. The six of us hunched over the coffee table, lifting our paper plates to our chins, sharing sausage-and-pepper pizzas.

My father wore his windpants and Patriots sweatshirt, and I was briefly reminded of happier, cozier winters—nights together, swaddled in flannel, indulging our mother when she switched the channel to figure skating.

At some point, she started swaying, bowing her head, humming while she chewed. Strands of her hair dipped into her soda cup and they resurfaced as one, thickened, like a tail. Dylan focused on his plate, calmly, in a way that suggested he'd done this before. My father cleared my mother's plate, though she wasn't finished. Then everyone started clearing their plates.

"Where are you going?" I asked abruptly, desperately, when Lia made her way out of the room.

"To smoke."

I followed her to the screened-in porch, though it was clear I wasn't welcome. Lia let the door slap behind her. Icicles cracked. Neon-colored floats lay deflated and creased on the ground. There were leftover beer cans from the previous summer, butts strewn on the floor. I suspected Lia had been out there all winter. Alone, most likely. Her college was only a thirty-minute drive away. She commuted from home.

She sat across from me at the round table, inspecting me, rotating an unlit cigarette between two fingers. Her nails were grown out, berry red. Her style had changed.

She laughed at the awkward silence, lit the cigarette, watched me through one eye as she took a drag.

"I can't feel my nose," I said, touching it with my fingertips.

"Go inside." She let the smoke drift languidly from her mouth, like she was putting on a show.

"Vera says hi."

"She's like this because of you."

"Who? Mom?"

She picked a piece of tobacco off her tongue.

"How can you say that?"

"Oh, go cry about it."

I had to try not to.

"We talk about you. Me and Sofia. About how you abandoned us."

Really? Soph? I didn't know if I should believe her. I thought of Sofia as a little girl, running around in her overalls, one buckle dangling by her leg. I tried to keep my voice steady, to push down the stone that was lodged in my throat.

Lia brushed her bangs from her eyes, something she did when she thought she was in charge. "You should do whatever you want. Live wherever. We're over it. But don't think for a second you're blameless."

"When have I ever said I'm blameless?"

She offered me her profile.

I leaned back in my seat, pretending to brush something off my coat. My hands were dry from the cold, and the zipper had nicked my finger. I sucked at the blood. Lia had a lot to say but she wasn't saying it. I wasn't going to encourage her either. I wasn't strong enough. I knew I was in the wrong.

She stabbed her cigarette on the table, fished inside her pack for another. My cold breath mingled with her smoke.

"She's killing herself," she said. "Look at her."

"And that's because of me?"

She studied the windows, the busted screens, packed thick with ice. "I don't know."

"Sofia seems happy," I said, to say something.

Lia agrees to change the subject, momentarily. "They're talking about moving in together, her and Dylan. She's been dating him for over a year." She brushed some ash from her coat. "But nothing is final. Mom doesn't even know it's a possibility. Are you still seeing that bartender?"

"No. He's an idiot."

"You think most people are idiots. Dad's the only one you don't talk down to."

"I don't talk down to you."

"If you talk to me at all."

She didn't know how lonely I'd been. "Do you, like, resent me or something?"

She laughed, loudly and with menace. "Jesus, Anna. Not everyone wants to move to *New York*." She leaned forward and her bracelets slid down her arms. "Not everyone wants to sleep with a different guy every night. There's nothing wrong with staying here. I'm going to grad school in the fall. I finished school early. You didn't know, because I didn't tell you, because you didn't ask. I'm going to have a life. It's just you who can't stand to be around this place."

"Yeah, because it's fucking suffocating. You used to think so too. You *hated* this house growing up."

"We were kids, Anna. We grew up. I'm not going to resent her forever. She's a person too. God, she's our fucking mother. And she's sick."

My tears made her angrier, like I knew they would.

"I'm not surprised it turned out this way," she said. "You never knew how to be the older sister." I didn't want to hear this. I'd only just walked in the door. "Don't you get it, Anna? It's not that you're in New York. It's that you never come back. You never check in. We're fucking nothing to you."

"You know that's not true." But how would she know?

"I'd feel too guilty leaving," she added. "Because I actually give a shit about other people." I didn't even have the chance to respond. She shot up from the table and let the screen door slam behind her.

I let her words roll around on my tongue, wanting to scream something back at her.

Sofia was a silhouette in front of the house, ponytail off to the side. "What are you guys doing out here?" she called into the snow, curious, oblivious. "It's freezing."

"I was smoking," I heard Lia say.

"Is Anna coming in?"

"Who fucking knows." She pushed past Sofia, who knew I needed something, that Lia and I had gotten into it, but she didn't know how or what to give. The distance between us was too great. I let that happen.

I didn't know my sisters anymore.

I didn't know Lia.

But I wanted to ask her:

Do you remember the night she left you at the playground? Your eyes squinting in the glare of headlights as she swooped around the lot? I cried for her to turn around but she said we had to teach you a lesson. She sped down pockmarked roads wearing only her nightgown and wool socks. A chalky patch of cereal milk blemishing the collar. I dug my nails into wet palms, angry with myself for not jumping out of the car right then, for not running and throwing my bigger arms around your smaller ones. We tore past the cornfields and onto the main road, where she unrolled the window, and let the wind whip her dirty curls, shouting about how you were going to be the end of her. You were *out of control.* In the backseat I tugged at my fingers, pinked and warmed, tugged with such force I thought they might pop from their sockets. I hated her for abandoning you but I didn't tell her this. I remember thinking you were going to freeze out there even though it was only October and you had on your windbreaker and your *Pocahontas* hat. I imagined finding you on the ground, eyes coated in mucus, lips blued. What would we do with you then? When we came back some minutes later you were standing by the swing set, toeing the dirt with your light-up sneakers. Your lower lip was thrusting out but I could see the swing shaking wildly behind you and I knew you'd just hopped off, that you only wanted her to think you'd been having a miserable time. She bopped the horn with her fist and you knew to come running. I could smell the cold coming off you when you slid in beside me. I took your hand.

Remember what she did that night? When we pulled into the garage and you crawled out from the backseat? She knelt bare-kneed on the concrete and pressed her face against your hard, little stomach, begged you not to tell him in her desperate whisper-strains. Her nails slipped as she clawed your coat. Tears puddled the fabric. You reached for a red hair strand. You took her in—her ruddy cheeks, lashes clumpy wet with mascara. I hadn't left the car but sank myself deeper into it, until I was crouched on the floor, my legs crumpled under the seat, afraid of her crying, of your mothering.

She did a lot of things back then but you seem to have

forgotten, judging by the hours you spend at her kitchen table. The afternoons you share over packaged pastries and coffee when I can barely manage a phone call.

Tell me, Lia, how do you forget?

Can you show me how it's done?

PART IV

Everett, Massachusetts

1984

She takes note of the things her mother has left behind—a beaded clutch for special occasions, a pair of espadrilles, a ladybug brooch. A chest of sweaters, a husband, a daughter. As the years mount to a decade, the girl decides it is easier to pretend her mother is dead, to pretend her leaving was not a choice. She decides this one rainy day at the cousins' while Julia lies on her stomach painting her nails Rum Raisin, swinging her legs while she sings to Billy Joel, little Charles crying because they've locked him out of the room, the smell of pasta e fagioli making its way through the closed door.

My mother did not leave me. My mother is dead.

31

In the late afternoon, the snow falls diagonally and sticks to the window screens. The house is darker than I remember. I linger in the front hall, taking in the woody smell. In the time I've been away, I've pictured her hundreds of times. The trick of bitterness has made certain things amplified, intensified. I envision too-big eyes, a tiny, flattened mouth, cartoonish.

I bring two coffees into the airless living room, where the overhead lights don't turn on. I see the lump of her shape, indistinct features shifting in the dimness.

"La dee da," she says, when I sit beside her. Her cane drops to the floor with a rattle. I place her coffee on the side table.

Can she feel the cold coming off my clothes? I wonder if she misses the outdoors, misses her birds and the feel of air. I haven't taken off my scarf or snow-speckled coat. I keep thinking about my jeans, still damp from the puddle at the train station. The hems are cool and crusted with street salt, brushing against my ankles.

"You going to turn on the light?" she asks.

I'd been afraid to. I pull the lamp string and my mouth opens in brief shock. I snap it shut. For a moment, she appears thinner. Half of her is in shadow. Her hair is light, sparse. I remember Sofia texting that my mother was lightening it, wanting the mix of auburn and gray to look more natural, but she wouldn't go to the salon. She does it out of a box, halfway, a smattering of left-over dye on the first-floor bathroom wall. Sofia helps her.

"What's new, Annie-Lou?" She laughs and loses her breath, making a horrible hacking sound. This makes her laugh harder. I make a move to get help but my father is outside in his nice trousers, knee-deep in the silent white, shoveling the path. He hasn't stepped foot in the house yet.

"Oh, don't bother," she says, in that graceless accent that stands out to me now. *Don't bawthah.* "It happens all the time."

"That's not good."

"It is what it is," she says. "What, no hugs for me?"

"Sorry," I mumble, moving forward. Wrapping my arms tentatively around her narrow shoulders, the feeling is unfamiliar. I drop back on the love seat, maybe too quickly. My elbows settle on the soiled arms and I'm thankful for the extra layer of clothing. It's the same cushion my sisters and I used to cram onto, three at a time. I rest my coffee in my lap, wait for my mother to speak.

My father says it's a fight getting her to take her vitamins. She looks older, worn, but mostly the same. Can't I go back? I want to go back. My eyes sting but I can keep control. Go back where?

"You like the new driveway lights?" my mother asks, not noticing my tears. "Your father put them in. I think they're too flashy but he says it's dangerous without them. Lia almost backed into him the other night." Her two front teeth jut over her lips, glinting in the lamplight.

"They're nice," I say.

"Not into the car. Into him." She pauses. "Imagine if that's how he goes," she says. "Flattened like a pancake in his own driveway. Imagine if he goes before me." She laughs.

"You went out to see the lights?" I ask.

"Saw a picture on their phone," she says, biting at the polish on her nails. "Like I said, too flashy. I like simple. Classy. Like my Christmas lights used to be."

I picture the holiday boxes in the attic—my mother's decorations, the Santas dressed in their mauve satin cloaks, the snowmen in their powder-blue caps. I picture those mechanical dolls, shifting and tilting and lifting their little candle lights. I'm not sure how simple or classy they were.

"Any boys?" my mother asks.

"No boys." I play with the plastic lid of my cup; I feel cold again.

My mother clicks her tongue, takes a sip of her coffee.

I unravel my scarf and yank it from my neck. The fabric burns. I need a break from this, just for a minute. I go into the kitchen. She calls after me. "Do you try? Do you go to the bars?" she asks. "Do you wear enough makeup? You're not rude, are you?"

"No." My fingertips skid atop waxy granite. There's rotting fruit in a bowl on the counter, bruised apples.

"Because you always had that attitude."

I take a breath.

"What about makeup, Anna? A pop of color goes a long way."

I might as well go back, if she's just going to keep talking.

"You're so sensitive sometimes. Your father and I used to hear you in high school, you know. Fighting on the phone with that Brandon until three in the morning." She was referring to my almost boyfriend in my senior year of high school. I cringe.

"One time—" My mother laughs at the ceiling. "One time, we were in bed and we thought we heard you crying on the front porch. So, your father ran down in his underwear—his little Fruit of the Looms—so he could go yell at some kid. Tell him to go the hell home. When he got down there it was just the neighbor's dog whimpering on the front steps."

As she laughs, her upper body shakes, like she's experiencing some kind of turbulence.

"I still think you need to go to the South to find a husband," she says, folding her hands on the pouch of her stomach. "A nice Southern gentleman."

"I'll be sure to consider it." I've never heard her say this.

"So. Tell me. Why'd you come home to your mother? Because he asked you to? I've been asking you for years. I always get an excuse."

"No, Mom. I wanted to come. I'm going upstairs for a minute," I say, lifting my duffel.

Her voice turns to gravel. "What'd he say about me? Is he complaining about me?"

"No."

"Tell me what he said." It's strange—the way we argue—as if no time has passed.

"He didn't say anything. I just came home."

"You're lying," she says, tapping her front teeth. "I can tell. Did something happen? You and Vera?"

"Please." I don't want to think about what I've done. Don't want to say the words out loud. How can she still know exactly how to get to me?

She mumbles something I can't make out.

"Dad says you're sick. What's wrong?"

"I have all kinds of pains. Don't sleep. The doctors think I fucked up with the pills. And then—" She interrupts herself to start laughing again, loudly, without measure. "And then I sure took a tumble down those garage steps."

I don't know how to respond to this mania, to this mother. I've lost the will, the compassion. As I walk through the foyer, I pass the big window. My father is still shoveling. He's slower to move, his back rounded all the way over. He takes a break every few seconds. On the drive home, he'd hunched over the steering wheel, squinting at the signs. Deep lines carved around his mouth. During the times I've seen him over the years, he's seemed frailer, as if he's also disappearing.

As I lug my duffel bag up the stairs, my mother calls out in a loud whisper, in that excited tone, "Wait, Anna, come look. *Come look.*"

She wants me to see the birds.

"Please, Anna. I promise it's worth it."

I throw my head back, groaning, pounding my feet down the steps.

I round the corner and my mother is attempting to hoist herself up. The leather creaks beneath her shifting weight. She waves a hand, motioning for me to come closer. "Be real, real quiet," she says. "Don't make any noise. See him?"

Outside, a wren lands on the bird feeder.

"Cool, Mom."

"Isn't he beautiful?"

"*So* beautiful."

"Isn't he though?"

It's an ordinary bird, dancing to shake snow off its head.

"Come on, Anna." She's winded, straining to look out the window. But she's happy. She could do this for hours.

"It's sweet," I say, and I give in, letting myself enjoy the moment. When the wren pushes off the bird feeder and flies away, I linger by her side and put my hand on her shoulder, hoping she'll know it's a sign of truce.

"Mom? Where are all the Christmas decorations?"

"I wasn't in the mood this year," she says.

"Are you in a lot of pain?"

"I told you I was," she says. "All the time."

She tells me my father has changed. He's become a better person.

She tells me I imagined it all—the damp spring morning we

found him passed out in the driveway, one leg hanging out of his truck. Even Trisha, though she doesn't say her name. She maintains that it was an animal that jumped in front of the car the night of the accident.

"It wasn't that bad," she tells me now. "You aren't remembering it right."

After everything he put her through, she's the one protecting him.

32

I knock on Lia's doorframe, slipping in before she can object. She's lying on her childhood bed with a hardcover propped on her stomach. The book jacket is on the floor. It's a rock memoir about some musician from the '90s.

"What do you want?" she says while still looking at her book.

"Can we be friends?"

Her hair is wet from the shower, her cheeks flushed. I can smell her coconut shampoo from across the room. I invite myself to sit at the bottom of her bed as she continues to ignore me. I wait for her to warm up, silently count the splattering of moles on her face.

She gives in. "What do you want, Anna?"

"You hate me."

"You couldn't even pick up the phone. You couldn't even do that."

I cross my legs, pull them close so I appear smaller.

"Sofia and I dealt with everything on our own. We're the reason she's even half coherent right now. Do you know how hard that was? It's not fair that you don't have to deal with any of this shit."

"It's hard for me to be around her. Even talk about her. I'm not saying it's easy for you. I'm just—more sensitive? I don't know. You're stronger." It sounds stupid when I say it out loud, like an excuse.

"Well, try harder. Because it's not easy for me. Or Sofia."

"I fucked up. I was being selfish. And I knew you'd take care of it." I look down when I say it, knowing I need to be a better person, a better sister.

"As long as you know," she says, raising the book to her face again.

"But I was also scared. I was afraid to find out what happened."

"Well, it's all over now."

"I know how much you did. Dad told me on the way here." I'm still embarrassed to say anything more sincere. "You think I've been having this amazing time in New York, but I'm miserable. I'm just like her. It terrifies me."

Her expression softens.

"I really am sorry."

"I know," she says. "We can be friends." She screws up her face, making fun of me.

There's a stuffed Eeyore tossed among her throw pillows. It's soft and plush, has a detachable tail. Bits of stray cotton cling to the Velcro. I smirk, holding the thing in the air. "Really?" It's from one of her old boyfriends.

"I know. I should have thrown that thing out."

"I guess he's kind of cute." She must have had this thing since she was fourteen. The kid she was seeing at the time had won it for her at the Topsfield Fair. She'd looked so grown-up that night, wearing a jean jacket and heeled boots, her arm looped through his. "Do you remember that night you came into my room? You were crying and covered in sand. I think you'd come from Gloucester and some guy had, like, forced you to do something?"

She stretches her legs out, eyeing her toe polish. "Why are you bringing that up?"

"I don't know. I think about it sometimes. I didn't realize how fucked-up the whole thing was until years later."

Lia gives me a look that tells me she's surprised. For a moment I regret saying it—thinking maybe I've offended her.

"I was jealous. You were lying there crying and I was mad it happened to you first."

She knocks her feet together. "Getting all deep on me now."

"I'm serious."

"It's not the craziest thing I've heard. I get it. I probably would have felt that way. If it was the other way around."

"You never really told me what happened that night."

She's uncomfortable. I can tell by the way she's smiling, self-mocking. "He didn't do it in a malicious way. I never actually said no."

"But he should have known."

"Oh, he knew." She finds the bookmark that's next to her leg, starts bending it between her fingers. "It was obvious through my body language and stuff. I don't get why any guy would want to have sex with a person who doesn't want to have it with them. How is that enjoyable?"

"I really am sorry."

"Anna. Stop. I haven't thought about that in years."

Sofia appears in the doorway. "Excuse me? Why wasn't I invited?" She jumps on the bed with her coat on, lies with her whole body across the mattress.

We sit that way for an hour or so, talking slow, settling into the old fluency.

"Do people tell you you're weird?" Lia asks me. "Like, your friends?"

"No, but now I'm a little concerned."

"It's not really a bad thing. You're just always talking about the past, worrying about the past."

"You're super serious," Sofia says, "Like, all the time."

Lia goes back to her book. "You should worry about the future. That shit's scary."

33

In the drawer of my mother's nightstand, beneath cotton pads, magazines, and the *Family Medical Guide,* there is an old photograph of my parents. They're in Portland, Maine, a month before their wedding, standing in a kitchen of knotty pine cabinets. On the countertops sit Heineken bottles and playing cards, a family of wooden ducks in a row. Through the window above the sink, you can see the seaside, hydrangeas and pasture roses swaying in the breeze.

My mother is at the center of the picture. She is wearing an oversized sweatshirt, blue-gray, with a small sailboat on the front. Her hair is all wild tresses, pulled away from her face in a tortoiseshell clip. Her cheeks glow a peachy pink. She is twenty-one and doesn't yet know the extent of her loss. Can't predict the frantic loneliness. What's most unusual about the photo is her posture—the playful slink of her body trying to escape. Her mouth is stuck in an O shape, gaping in gleeful protest as my full-bearded father comes at her, one hand grasping her waist, the other holding a wriggling lobster.

I take deep sips of water at the kitchen island while my mother and sisters sit on the couch, grabbing from the popcorn bowl, gazes bewitched by the flashing television.

I hate the itching, squirming feeling of being trapped in this house. It's only been a few days, but it's somehow worse than New York. I want to call Vera, confide in her. I've lost the right. I think of our few exchanges. The number of times I've told her I'm sorry, desperately, text after text. She responded with one line: *I know.* Somehow, this gives me hope.

I wait until my sisters head upstairs to bed. Then I join my mother. She's listening to the television while browsing the iPad in her hands. "It's late," she says, glancing at the clock on the cable box. "You're like me."

"No, I'm not."

"I knew it since you were real little. The time you were playing with the dead parakeet."

"Jesus." I slip onto the cushion. "I wasn't playing with it."

"Sorry. Watching TV with it."

My mother likes to tell this story—when I snuck down to the cellar to get our parakeet, Larry, out of the storage freezer where my father had stashed him postmortem. I didn't like picturing him all alone. He sat in my lap while I watched *Judge Judy*, cold and stiff, claws scrunched up like dried flowers.

"Well. You should go to bed," she says to me. "It's not good to be up so late."

I let out a small laugh. "You're one to talk."

"Will you help me with this?" she holds up the iPad. "I need to buy skin stuff. To make me look younger."

I take the iPad from her, start scrolling through the beauty website she's pulled up.

"I need collagen. Click on that."

"You don't need that. Just get a serum."

"I do. I need to boost my collagen. They told me I do."

"Who told you?"

"That's what they say. You need collagen to look youthful."

"Who's 'they'?"

"Everyone, Anna!"

"Okay, okay. You can have your collagen." I add it to her online basket, hand her the iPad. "I'm going to head up." I make a move to stand.

"Wait. Don't." She tugs my wrist, startling me with her touch, so much so that I pull away out of instinct. She looks hurt. I want to reverse the moment, give my wrist back. "Don't leave," she manages to say.

"You're being weird. What is it?" I give her the eyes, telling her to say what she wants to say.

"I'll never know the answer," she says, pretending to scroll on her iPad. "Why my own daughter hates me so much."

I don't want to have this conversation, but I collapse next to her anyway. We need to have this conversation.

"You know I don't hate you."

"You could show it sometimes," she says, tight-lipped, like she doesn't really want me to hear. "You act so ungrateful."

"Because I have so much to be grateful for."

"What, you wanted to be smothered in kisses? Wanted me to hold your hand through life?"

"Mom. I'm tired." I raise my face to the ceiling.

She tosses the iPad aside, coughs into her nightgown sleeve.

"I'm sorry," I muster. "I know it was hard for you. Growing up without a mother, practically raising us alone. Moving out here. Dad gave me the speech in the car."

My mother searches the walls, as if there is a hidden message to be deciphered there. She doesn't respond to my apology. I can't be sure she's heard it.

"Okay, then." I get up to leave.

"Will you just sit?"

I raise a brow.

"My mother didn't get sick. She didn't die. I don't think."

It takes me a moment to realize what she's said. I'm not sure I've heard her right. Again, I take a seat.

My mother goes quiet for a few seconds, seeming to choose her words. "We had this big field in the back of our house right by the old peanut factory. I showed you one time. Dirty, filthy field. Thousands of dandelions. Half dead from the pollution. We would go out there after early suppers to pick them, the two of us. Me and my mother. We'd make dandelion crowns. Little bracelets. She liked those flowers. Even the broken ones.

"She got so strange towards the end. Neglectful, even. Always falling into dark moods. She wouldn't even look at me sometimes. It got to the point where she didn't want me to say a word, never mind sit in the same room. I was eight, maybe nine years old."

She takes in a long breath, plays with the hem of her nightgown.

"I was sitting in the front parlor while they were going at it one weekend—my mother and father. I don't remember what it was all about. He was smashing things. She was just standing still, not doing a thing, letting him go crazy. He must have passed out on the sofa because she went to her bedroom after that.

"I went in there and started poking, pulling on her arm. I wanted her to get out of the house—to see the birds, to feel the sun. Maybe it would make her feel better. So I opened up the curtains. I brought her shoes to the bed. I kept pulling until she sat up. Eventually it worked. We had a big bag with us, and I was going through the rows of dandelions, picking them. I was being careful. Wanted to make sure they didn't tear. We were there for a while, and I guess I went off on my own.

"I was singing as I went, waiting for her voice to match with mine. It must have been a Sunday because not many of the neighbors were out. Usually you could hear them talking, hollering at each other from their porches. Without them distracting me, I just kept going, kept singing. But I couldn't find her voice, started to hear it coming from different directions. It wasn't until I reached the chain-link fence, hundreds of feet away, that I realized it was only my voice I could hear."

She held herself firmly, speaking with a kind of deliberateness, a conscious control I hadn't heard from her in years. It was like she was in a trance.

"The bag of flowers was almost full and I looked around, saw how far I'd gone, was wondering why she hadn't yelled for me. It was a big, big field. The sun was so bright, making it hard to see, to walk. I turned to my left, my right, was calling for her. Running this way and that. I went back and forth to the house and the field, calling and calling. I ran to nearby streets. Checked neighbors' porches to see if she'd run into somebody, got stuck talking. I must have run around for an hour.

"I don't know," she continues. "I don't know why she did it. I waited in the middle of the field that whole day. Until the sun went down. My father never came looking for me. Or her. 'Let her do what she wants.' That's what he said when I came inside. It's all he kept saying."

Her face is calm, accepting. "I guess she was sick of it all. She had left before, once or twice, but she always came back the same night. It was her perfume that would wake me. It'd wake me right up. I used to try to find it in the stores but could never remember the name."

"Where did she go?"

"She could be anywhere. Or maybe not. Maybe she died. Who knows."

"But what made her do it?" I was getting frustrated. I needed more.

"My father, probably. I used to have dreams. Of her peering through the bedroom window. I haven't had them in years."

"Does anyone know why? I mean, the old neighbors? Her

friends? How could you never find out what happened?" I hear the accusation in my voice, but I can't help it, I want to find her, save her, bring her back to my mother.

She frowns. "My mother never really had friends. Her family—my grandparents—had already passed. It was me and my mother and my father. Always."

"Maybe we can find her."

She shakes her head. "She'd be seventy-eight now? Seventy-nine? I don't even know her birthday. Imagine that?"

"We can ask around—"

"There'd be no point. She missed a whole life. Lives. You girls. What's even the point? To go looking for someone that doesn't want to be found?"

I feel cold, deflated. "Does Dad know?"

"He knows."

"Does anyone else?"

"I'm sure some people remember. Everett people. Those that are left. I don't know. It's embarrassing. You don't want to tell people your mother left you. Mothers don't leave. It's fathers who leave." She runs her hands over her lap. "I waited a long time, though. A part of me thought she might come back someday."

It hits me that perhaps this was her reasoning for not wanting to leave Everett.

I have questions, details that don't add up, but I won't interrogate her. It's not difficult for me to understand why she preferred her mother be dead. What's harder is the secret. The knowledge that you can never really know a person. The knowing that someone can walk away from you, forever.

I think of the flowers, my mother, the flowers, her sorrow spreading through the rooms of this house wildly and uncontrollably, like a weed.

34

They say that animals experience grief over the loss of their companions. They can even see their loved ones when they aren't there. Wolves will wander in the night, independent from the rest of the pack. They will howl to themselves, tails coiled between their legs. Caught in the space between having and losing, they will stroll in a figure eight, as if pleading for the dead.

When I wake in the blue of morning, a feeling wrenches me from sleep, an invisible fist clutching, yanking me upward. I can't focus with my heart trying to flee, with warm air cloistered around my head. The sheets are wet, drenched in the shape of me. They cling to my back and thighs. When I push the sheets to the floor, a violent sob escapes me, so loud I'm sure I've woken someone.

I need to go. With my packed bag on my arm, I move through the hallway, engulfed in a buzzing silence. The hall night-lights flicker when I pass. It's too quiet, too hot, the heat in the house is on too high. I'm overwhelmed with a need to run. Before I know it, I'm rushing down the staircase, past the kitchen, past my mother on the couch. She's cloaked in a green blanket, her body moving slowly, a shelled animal.

I open the sliding doors and step into the yard. It's white and disorienting. Almost blinding. I keep going until I reach the place where the snow drifts into dirt, where the ground plummets into the pit. I sit with my legs dangling over the edge. My head tilts, releasing tears.

A gust of snow drifts from the white in the sky to the white on the ground. The air is thin. I'll never get enough. My lungs are scraped. I gasp again.

I can't tell where the earth and sky begin.

The yard is barren of sound.

No birds. No murmuring of leaves. Even the rushing of wind is faint. It's like I'm shielded beneath an invisible dome. It's what I love and hate the most about this place—the silence, so deep you can hear it.

I waver here, the strap of my duffel digging a ravine into my shoulder. The forest is somewhere to my right. I don't know what's in there, but surely it leads to something. Surely something better than this. I could keep walking. I could get onto the road.

As I consider this, dawn breaks, trees crackle and shake.

Go through the woods. Get onto the road.

Take the first train.

Go through the woods.

There's a sound behind me.

Get onto the road.

A rustling.

Take the train.

Go through the woods.

Get onto the road.

A heavy crunching.

Take the train.

Go through the woods.

Faint enough for me to ignore.

Get onto the road.

Take the train.

Go through the woods.

Get onto the road.

Take the train.

Turning back to the house, I see her coming toward me through a haze. Her eyes are wide and white as the snow. The blanket dangles from her shoulders while she stabs the ground with her cane, her left arm dangling. I call out to her, asking her to stop, telling her she'll fall. Her cheeks are splotched red, her temples pearled with sweat, but she keeps coming. When she reaches me, she grips my shoulder, teeters to the ground. Her lips have blued. There are several seconds of me listening to her rasping breath, mechanic when it catches in her throat.

"What, you were going to walk to New York?" she says. The blanket clings to her and she discards it, exposing the rest of her to the cold. She's wearing only a nightgown and slippers.

I'm crying, the giant pit becoming a smudge through my tears.

Around us, the evergreens blink in the morning light, dripping. We're quiet again for a long time, until there's a feeling of ease. She isn't saying anything, isn't looking at me. She's staring into the hole that seems to have deepened. I turn back to the house and that's when I see it—a little wren perched on the ice-filled bath. He pecks at the frozen surface, looks around, pecks again, looks around. Sends out a plaintive chirp.

"Diana," I say, nodding in the direction of the bird.

Her fingertips grasp the packed snow as she turns slowly, unsteadily. Another breath catches in her throat. She looks at the bird, not smiling or frowning. She's just there, and despite everything, she's who I care for most. She looks on, settling. Wind whips at our backs. The wren sings.

Acknowledgments

Thank you to my agent, Alice Whitman, who pushed me to delve deeper and made me a better writer. Equal thanks to my editor, Laura Perciasepe, for her unmatchable insight and critical eye. I am supremely grateful to have such brilliant women behind this novel. My sincere gratitude also to Alison Fairbrother and the rest of the Riverhead and Cheney teams.

I'm indebted to those who championed this novel for so many years, reading countless drafts and offering honest, invaluable critique: Olaya Barr, Lillian Klein, Crystal Hana Kim, Katrine Øgaard Jensen, and Sanaë Lemoine. To Dana Isernio, for her unyielding encouragement, and for the hours spent revising these chapters in our Morningside Heights apartment all those years ago.

Thank you to my parents, Lisa and Paul Maiuri, for their faith and love as I journeyed onto the writer's path. And to Lauren Aghoian and Nina Maiuri, my first best friends and lifelong confidantes. I am so lucky to call you my home.